The *painting* was Nick's. The *agent* was Nick's. But the signature on the painting *wasn't* Nick's. . . .

Nick took the magazine for a closer look. His reaction was like a double take from a silent film. His brows drew together and he made a strangled "argh" sound. "*It's mine!* That's my *Rouge et Noir* study! The son of a bitch!"

"Oh, no," Nancy said firmly, "that's definitely a Frageau. I recognize the brushwork. Remember, Lana, we were wondering how he did it, and I thought he used a very full brush, with a ruler to build up that dynamic edge of impasto—unusual with acrylics. It's more common with oils."

Nick continued staring at the reproduction. "To hell it's a Frageau. It's mine. And I didn't use a ruler. I used masking tape."

Nancy examined the picture again. "It says Frageau," she said, pointing out the signature.

"I don't care if it says Picasso! I know my own work. He's painted over my signature. . . ."

Jove Books by Joan Smith

THE POLKA DOT NUDE
CAPRICCIO
A BRUSH WITH DEATH
FOLLOW THAT BLONDE

FOLLOW THAT BLONDE

JOAN SMITH

JOVE BOOKS, NEW YORK

FOLLOW THAT BLONDE

A Jove Book / published by arrangement with
the author

PRINTING HISTORY
Jove edition / August 1990

ISBN: 0-515-10384-5

Jove Books are published by The Berkley Publishing Group,
200 Madison Avenue, New York, New York 10016.
The name "JOVE" and the "J" logo
are trademarks belonging to Jove Publications, Inc.

PRINTED IN THE UNITED STATES OF AMERICA

10 9 8 7 6 5 4 3 2 1

FOLLOW THAT BLONDE

CHAPTER 1

My blouse clung like damp tissue to my back. Wet spaghetti strands of hair glued themselves to my fevered brow, and the blister on my little toe was bleeding. I know—you're supposed to wear comfortable, flat-heeled shoes for sight-seeing, but the sights we had in mind when we left the hotel were the fancier shops along the Via Condotti, and you don't wear sneakers there. Not that either Nancy or I planned to add to our wardrobe at Bulgari's or Gucci's, but when in Rome . . . And that's where we were—determined to see it all during the few hours of the day that anything was open. Where we were not, unfortunately, was within view of the Via Condotti.

We were in one of those narrow, cobblestoned alleys that run like capillaries through the city, leading nowhere. The rough paving hated my heeled sandals, but not as much as I hated Rome. And I had looked forward to it so! Paris and Rome were supposed to be the highlights of our trip. Paris was great, very French, very enjoyable, very expensive. Rome turned out to be a crumbling, disjointed, unfriendly old jumble of a place, with a few new buildings sticking out like brass buttons on a shroud. Pisa had no monopoly on leaning buildings. The slanting walls of the houses in this alley practically met overhead. They looked ready to tumble down on us at any moment. On the façade beside us there was a mosaic of the Virgin held in an oval frame with a card stuck in it advertising shoe repairs on the floor above. It

1

struck me as fairly typical of Rome: a lot of religiosity, tinged with commerce. In the doorway, two cats lapped pasta from a tin plate.

When we came to the next corner, Nancy Bankes grabbed my elbow and pointed left. "There—that looks like a real street," she said hopefully, and we headed toward it. At the intersection there was an Italian traffic policeman in white helmet and gloves, doing his imitation of Baryshnikov, bowing and mincing and throwing his arms around as cars and motorcycles whizzed past. It *was* a real street, and I girded my toes for another block of torture.

A block past the traffic cop, we stumbled out into searing sunlight and a blaze of expensive boutiques. We had already done the requisite Rome-tourist things with our tour group: been awestruck by St. Peter's, thrown our French change into the Fountain of Trevi (before I learned this presaged a return to Rome!). No doubt the charm wouldn't work. Nothing else did, including the telephones. We had visited churches, toured the Colosseum, visited more churches, been jostled up and down the Spanish Steps and admired the view, had our *aperitivi* at outdoor cafés, visited more churches. Nancy's eminently pinchable bottom was black and blue from Italian "compliments." My pristine white cellulite was slightly marked. What I had especially wanted to see, we had missed. It had poured rain the evening we were supposed to see the Sound and Light show at the Forum. Fortunately, our group rescheduled the trip for tonight.

I dug a Band-Aid out of my big purse and leaned against a storefront to apply it, while Nancy cased the pedestrians for hunks. One of them "accidentally" bumped against her and stopped to apologize profusely in incomprehensible Italian before I got the Band-Aid on. There are hazards to travelling with a Nancy Bankes. Nature had endowed my cousin with all the charms that ensure survival of the species, viz a mane of tangled blond hair, big green eyes with lashes a yard long, pouty lips, a warm, gullible personality, and the kind of figure that is currently out of fashion but never goes out of style.

Opposites attract. It is a continuing humiliation that my mother named me Lana, after the movie star. I was such a pretty baby, she says, and the family album supports this unlikely fact. Blond curls have faded to mouse, streaked back to blond when I get around to it, which I did for this European tour. My blue eyes prefer glasses to contacts. I bought a pair of prescription-tinted glasses for this trip, to lighten the image of the school teacher. My cute little dimpled baby's body has stretched to five feet, eight inches, reasonably fleshed, but lacking the sort of curves that cause Italian pedestrians to lose their balance.

"You're lucky," Nancy often says. "If I so much as *smell* chocolate, I put on a pound." What she doesn't say is that the extra weight goes to all the right places. She has a nineteen-inch waist, which accentuates the thrust of bosoms above, the flare of hips below. She's not perfect, however. Her ankles are fat, whereas I have the slender, bony underpinnings of a thoroughbred.

I got the Band-Aid on, and Nancy and I went whispering and giggling like a couple of hicks into the expensive *-ucci* boutiques—Gucci, Pucci—to be condescended to by the clerks. In Bulgari's, Nancy's smile got the man to actually unlock a big sapphire ring from the glass-fronted counter and let her try it on, with a guard hovering nearby. She pretended not to realize the clerk was hitting on her, but I'm sure she recognized such words as *bella, telefono, albergo*, and *ristorante*. God knows she'd heard them often enough the past week. What hampered her understanding was that she was becoming involved with our tour guide, Ron Evereton. Nancy wants to get married, and certainly will. She could get hit on at a Girl Guides Convention.

"*Grazie, signore,*" she said with a smile, and we left, ringless of course, to continue our window shopping.

"I'd like to get back to that Via dei Coronari where they have the antique shops," I said. "There was an old silver filigree necklace there I'd like to buy. Let's try to find a taxi. I can't walk another step."

Nancy wrinkled her nose. She doesn't approve of antiques. Our tastes are quite dissimilar. "It's this way," I said, and we walked some more, beyond that charmed circle where traffic is limited to essential vehicles, of which there seem to be an inordinate number.

"An *aperitivo*?" she suggested, knowing my weakness. "We have time. We're not meeting the group for dinner till seven-thirty. Gee, I wish we could stay longer than four days. You can't begin to see Rome in four days," she pouted.

A batch of umbrella-shaded tables lured us across the street. I sat down and eased my swollen toes out of my sandals. "Campari and soda, *per piacere*."

"Make that *due*," Nancy said, smiling.

The waiter took a peek down her scoop-necked blouse (that was mostly scoop) before leaving. We were sitting under our red and white striped umbrella, sipping Camparis, feeling very tired and hot and continental, when I saw him. With the innate viciousness of the young, we used to call Bert "Pig Eyes" at school. He had sharp green eyes with sparse lashes and an upturned nose. If he had been popular, we would probably have thought him cute, but Bert was never popular. He tried too hard, and he wore the wrong clothes.

"That's Bert Garr!" Nancy exclaimed excitedly.

I suppose every high school gang has a Bert Garr. Despite the fact that nobody really liked him, he had somehow wheedled his way into our group with an unpleasant mixture of groveling, maneuvering, determination and sheer nerve on his part, and apathy on ours. When a party was being planned, he'd volunteer to do whatever unpleasant job needed to be done, to make sure he was included. He was good at getting bargains—records, stereos—as he always knew someone that would give him a discount. Then, too, we felt a little sorry for him, but as sure as you were nice to him, he'd turn around and use you in some way.

I looked down the street at the blond man hustling along, ogling some girls. Bert had always been a hustler. He still looked like one, although he had upgraded his clothes. Today he wore a decent shirt, blue and white stripes, with blue trousers and expensive Italian loafers. He was wearing sunglasses, too. I hadn't recognized him at first, but as he got closer, I realized it was him all right, thinned down, with a more stylish haircut. The last time I'd seen him was the summer he graduated from Benjamin Franklin High, a year before I did. He had long hair then, and zits. He kept looking over his shoulder now, and the fast walk turned into a run, as if somebody was chasing him. Nobody in his right mind would run in weather like this.

"What can he possibly be doing here?" I mused. "Didn't he get a job in New York after high school?"

"That was ages ago." Nancy stood up and began waving and shouting. "Bert! Bert Garr, over here."

Bert stopped, looked all around. For a minute, I had the strange feeling he was frightened or something. He looked back, searching the throng on the sidewalk. Nancy shouted again and he spotted us. A smile split his face and he came pouncing down on us. I took a quick peek at the passing crowd, but no one seemed to be paying any attention to Bert.

"Nancy Bankes. I don't believe it! If you aren't a sight for sore old Yankee eyes."

Before he could pull her off her chair and into his arms, she shook his hand. "Wow. Talk about synchronicity!" Nancy beamed. She had been reading Carl Jung, and was much caught up in synchronicity that summer. From what I could figure out, this synchronicity was a blend of ESP and coincidence, although Jung (and Nancy) clothed it in loftier terms.

"And we didn't even set our watches." Bert's use of idiom was always a little off. As an English teacher, I found this about as grating as a fingernail scraped over a blackboard. "Nice to see a face from home. Can I join you, buy you ladies a drink?" He sat down and examined me. "Is that you, Lana?" He pulled his glasses down and peered over them.

"Hi, Bert. Fancy meeting you here." We shook hands. Time had improved Bert's looks. The zits had left no marks behind. His pink skin had tanned to café au lait, and his figure was now good.

He tossed his head at the waiter. "*Vino secco, bianco per favore*, Mac." He hooked his elbows over the back of his chair, arched out his chest, crossed one leg over the other, and smiled. His manner hadn't changed. Still trying to act as if he owned the world. I noticed the loafers were worn down at the heels. "So what brings you ladies to the Eternal City?"

"We're making a four-week tour—England, France, Italy, Spain, and Portugal," Nancy explained.

"The Latin lap. Too bad you settled for the cheap one. Germany and Belgium are worth a gander. Very clean. So you're ladies of leisure, I see. You must have married doctors." He checked out Nancy's left hand and, as an afterthought, mine.

"No, we're still single," Nancy said. "We both teach at Benjamin Franklin High. Lana teaches English; I teach Art."

"Oh, teaching. It figures. So you're both still back in little old Troy," he said, shaking his head in a patronizing way that suggested he was now the C.E.O. of some international corporation. "What's keeping that waiter?"

"Are you married, Bert?" Nancy asked with a hungry eye.

"Who, me?" He laughed. "No way, José."

"What are you doing here?" I asked. Whatever it was, I knew it would be insignificant, possibly borderline illegal, and he'd make it sound as if he were running the country.

"I guess you'd call it P.R. I have a stable of artists. I do their publicity, manage some of 'em. Kind of an agent." He took off his sunglasses and began sucking one end.

"What do you mean?" Nancy asked. "Like, performing artists, or what?"

"No, *real* artists, guys that paint pictures. If you can't beat 'em, join 'em."

"Are you an artist?" Nancy asked, ready to find synchronicity lurking. I knew better. Bert sprinkled clichés with a fine lack of discrimination, like salt on French fries.

"Not an artist per se. More of an appreciator."

"Do you live here, in Rome?"

"I've got to be some place. I finally settled down in Rome."

"Weren't you working in New York?" Nancy asked, frowning.

Bert rolled his eyes skyward. "You're talking ancient history, Nance. I've done it all since then. I did some marketing for Pan-Am in the Big Apple." I mentally translated this to selling tickets. "Did a lot of globe-trotting—freebies. I worked for a travel agency for a while, and finally I decided to be a guide. Why not put my experience to use? When I got tired of the old If-it's-Tuesday-it-must-be-Belgium routine, I put up my tent on the banks of the Tiber. Time to put down some roots." He uncrossed his legs and planted his run-down loafers firmly on the pavement.

"How did you become an artist's agent?" Nancy asked. It was a reasonable question. I'd be surprised if Bert knew a Michelangelo from a marshmallow.

"A guy gets around," he said vaguely. "When I was a tour guide, I used to go through the galleries a lot with the people we hired to herd the gang. Culture—I figure it wouldn't do me any harm. I learned about chiaroscuro, impasto, perspective—all that artistic jazz." Nancy nodded her approval. "Boy, if I ever have to look at that Mona Lisa again, I'll barf. Talk about your bow-wows. Now this exhibit I've mounted— Hey! I'm just on my way there now." He leaned forward eagerly. "I'm meeting my main man. Wanna come along and meet a real artist?" He did a quick scan of the street as he spoke. I had that uncomfortable feeling again that Bert was being followed. Was he inviting us along to protect him?

Nancy said, "Wow! Super, huh, Lana?"

"Your wine hasn't come yet, Bert," I reminded him.

"Forget it. If they don't want my lire, I'll keep them."

Nancy began to gather up her purse. I had visions of some hole-in-the-wall den, hung with amateurish scrawls designed to gouge money from tourists. "It's getting a little late," I said.

"It's only four-thirty," Bert pointed out. He lifted his arm and flashed a Gucci watch, one of those ones with the red and green striped face. I noticed chrome showing below the gilt paint on the edges. "Gucci," he said, then snorted. "A knockoff. A man over on Via Condotti can get them for five sawbucks, and he still makes fifty percent on every deal, but you didn't hear it from this guy. Imagine what Gucci, Inc., makes. So, are you gals coming along or what?"

"My feet are bleeding," I said.

"We'll share a taxi," Nancy suggested. "Where's the gallery, Bert?"

"You could hop to it on one foot from here. It's not exactly a gallery," he said. My spirits sank. More cobble-stoned alleys. "I've hired the exhibition room at the Quattrocento Hotel."

Bert could still surprise. The ancient grandeur of the Quattrocento—Bert Garr? It was like a rock concert at the Vatican. The Quattrocento was not only respectable, it was downright prestigious. This I had to see. "Just let me stick another Band-Aid on my toe. This one's coming off already."

"You should wear comfortable, flat-heeled shoes for rubbernecking," Bert said. "I always told my group to."

I fixed my Band-Aid while Bert and Nancy talked about the old days in Troy. He placed some bills on the table. "My treat, I insist," he said grandly, and ruined the gesture by adding, "even if I didn't have anything to drink." With one hand on Nancy's elbow, the other on mine, he hurtled us along to the hotel.

I wondered if we'd be invited to leave when I got a look at the old marble floor, the soaring ceiling, the antique statues, and gilt and plush everything else in the lobby. It was one of those hushed places where you could hear a diamond drop. Bert's slightly nasal twang echoed. "This place is considered *très* chic, believe it or not. I'll take a nice new Hilton any day, but Nick—that's my man—prefers this joint. We opened last week—too bad you weren't here. We had champagne and caviar and everything. We even had a contessa drop in."

I assumed the Contessa was one of Bert's embroideries,

an assumption which was wrong. He led us down a marble corridor to the exhibition room. It had double doors, both opened. A marble and gilt table at the entrance held about fifty pounds of fresh flowers in huge urns. A young man sat at a table with brochures and papers in front of him. Bert called him Alberto, and talked to him for a minute in Italian, with a sprinkling of English. A quiet crowd moved about, examining the pictures. This was no tourist rip-off. The people had that old world, old money air about them. Their voices were discreetly low, and they were actually examining the pictures. I decided that what Bert really did here was take turns with Alberto, guarding the door. Our lack of Italian would keep us in the dark.

"Have a gander, ladies. I'll be right back," Bert said, and faded into the crowd. We went in and gazed all around. There were no scrawls, no wild blobs of modern art here. The paintings were serenely beautiful landscapes of the Italian countryside. The skill of the artist was unmistakable. Maybe genius wasn't too strong a word to use. I felt the hair on the back of my neck move, the way it lifts in homage to a true masterpiece. The scenes were varied: some of them rough, geometric Tuscany countryside, more of them gently rolling hills of Umbria, with ancient farmhouses tucked into valleys or hanging from the mountainside. There were figures of people in some of them, bent old women in black gowns and men with medieval faces. One painting was of an olive orchard with boys in the gnarled, misshapen trees, shaking them. Nets were spread under the trees to catch the harvest. The surface was so smooth, almost transparent, as if the painting had grown on the canvas. "Tempera," Nancy explained. "Not many work in that medium nowadays. Wyeth does, back home. It's very difficult. You can tell the artist really loves Italy. I wonder if he's here."

I was wondering if Bert even *knew* him. How could such a sensitive man tolerate Bert Garr for his agent? I saw Bert talking to a tall, slender man in a white suit, and knew the man was the artist. At least he looked the way an Italian artist should look. Silky black hair grown rather long, just touching his shirt collar. One ruler-straight lock fell over his forehead. His eyes were like black velvet, softly passionate. His cheeks were lean and tanned, rather ascetic, and his expression sensitive. He gestured with his long-fingered, El Greco hands, his arms, his whole body, but in a lazy, langorous way, as if the world was not to be taken too seriously. Bert, wearing a harried frown, was talking a mile a minute. The man looked mildly bemused.

I edged closer. The artist was speaking now to a red-faced man in a clerical collar. His dulcet voice, smooth and luxurious as cashmere sounded lovely. I thought Bert must have pointed Nancy and me out to him, because as the priest answered, the artist's dark eyes moved occasionally toward us, wearing a gleam of interest. Nancy, being only five feet, one inch, couldn't see over the intervening heads.

"A lot of this stuff is sold already," she pointed out. "And look at the prices! Of course it's quoted in lire, but even so . . ."

"How did Bert ever latch on to this man?" I asked. It was a rhetorical question, but Nancy answered, in a huffy voice.

"What do you mean? Bert was always a go-getter. He was voted the most likely to succeed in our yearbook."

"He was voted the most likely to become a millionaire or end up in jail," I reminded her. I trust she needed no reminding of the reason for the addendum. When Bert, the crook, was Treasurer of the Student Council, there were invariably shortfalls, which he disguised by some accounting cosmetic surgery. Mysterious entries appeared in the books. Like entertainment for advertising purposes, but none of the local stores or companies were accustomed to being wooed into their twenty-five dollar contributions to the yearbook. Transportation suddenly appeared in the accounts. (Bert's usual transportation was a bicycle.) Certainly he pocketed part of our money, hard earned by selling chocolate bars door to door. And now he had graduated to cheating this beautiful, innocent artist of part of his earnings. As sure as God made green apples, Bert was running some scam.

"You never did like Bert," she accused.

"Neither did anybody else."

The awful truth was out before I remembered that Nancy had gone out with him for a while. I've already indicated our tastes are different. We were never best friends, but as cousins in the same grade through school, we saw a lot of each other. And now that we were both teaching at Ben Franklin, we were together five days a week. Which still doesn't explain why she went out with Bert. I never could understand it, although he lived on her block, and since he was a little older, maybe she had some carry-over of hero worship. She could have had anyone, but she went out with Bert for about a month, and even then I think he broke it off. It was around the time Bert graduated.

The cleric wandered off. Bert got hold of the artist's elbow and began rushing him over to meet us. I felt suddenly shy. I wished I had paid more attention to the dog-eared Berlitz phrasebook in my purse.

"Gals, this is my man, Nickie. A regular Michelangelo."

Nickie—Niccolò. A fine old Italian name. *"Piacere della—"* Oh lord, what came next? I smiled and hunched my shoulders apologetically.

"Pleased to meetcha." Niccolò smiled, and pumped my hand firmly. Not a trace of Italy in his accent, although he had been speaking Italian earlier. There was something different, possibly an echo of Boston. Was this langorous Adonis an American?

Bert continued with the introductions. Nick Hansen. That was the man's name. From Boston, Massachusetts. Via Paris at least, to lend him an aura of glamor.

"Your work is just *fabulous,* Nick," Nancy told him. "I'm green with envy. I'm an artist, too, sort of. I teach the plastic arts in Troy."

Nick's liquid eyes performed a surreptitious examination of her charms, and a soft smile of admiration lifted his lips. "We'll have to get together and compare notes. Bert's told me so much about you."

I mumbled a mild compliment. "Your painting is lovely, Nick."

"Thank you," he said politely, and even pried his eyes loose from Nancy long enough to flicker a quick, disinterested glance over me. Bert, it seemed, had not told him anything about me.

"Hey, it's nearly five bells," Bert said. "What do you say we leave the shop to Alberto, have a few drinks, and chow down? Show the gals some *cucina romana*. I know a place, ladies . . ."

"Our group is meeting at seven-thirty to go out for dinner," I explained. "We really should be getting back to our hotel."

Bert wagged his head knowingly. "I know these tour meals. Do yourselves a favor and skip it. Clip joints. By the time the proprietor and guide have taken their slice, you end up paying twice what a plate of pasta's worth."

"We could phone the hotel," Nancy suggested. Nancy would cancel a trip to the moon for a date.

"We really should get back. After dinner and the Sound and Light show tonight we're catching a bus with the group to our hotel in Naples," I explained to Bert and Nick.

"Naples," Bert scoffed. "They'll stable you at Capua and *commute* you to Naples for the tours. Cheaper."

"No, we'll be staying at Naples, and we've already paid," I pointed out. "Our reservations have been made. We already missed the Sound and Light show at the Forum once," I added.

"We've seen the Forum—in passing, I mean," Nancy reminded me. "It's just another old shambles."

"We'll take you to the Forum after dinner," Bert said. "I know the place inside-out. I must have been trailed through it umpteen times with the guide when I was touring with my group."

Maybe if Nick had been a real Italian, maybe if he'd been smiling at me instead of Nancy, maybe if the old friend had been anyone but Bert Garr, whose offer to show us the Forum wasn't worth the paper it wasn't written on, I might have gone along with it. No way was I going to spend the next four hours listening to Bert boast and abuse the Queen's English.

"Well, that's that then," Nancy said, with a commanding glare at me. "Bert will show us the Forum after dinner."

I glared her down. "Everything is arranged with the group."

Bert wasn't listening. His attention had strayed to the doorway, where a slender beauty had just entered. She wore her long, honey-colored hair in a chignon. As I stared, she reached up a hand with long, bloodred fingernails and removed a pair of yellow-tinted glasses, which seemed redundant in Italy, but looked interesting. Her dress was elegantly simple, a gray linen sheath with white piping, and she breathed class and money. About ten fine gold bracelets tinkled discreetly on her left arm. At the end of her shapely legs she wore high-heeled green snakeskin sandals designed to destroy her arches forever. There were no Band-Aids on her toes.

"Holy Christ, that's the Contessa! She's come back!" Bert exclaimed. I had to accept that I'd misjudged him again. A contessa really had attended the opening of this show. She had probably drunk champagne and eaten caviar, and Bert apparently really was the artist's manager. "She's always in the papers. She's a collector. If we could palm one of your pix off on her— What's her name, Nick? Fettucini, Linguini—something to do with pasta."

"Lingini," Nick said, with a tolerant smile at Bert's butchered pronunciation.

"Right, Lingini," Bert said, and pelted forward to glad-hand her. Her questioning, aristocratic look of surprise deterred him not a whit. He went on chatting and grinning as if he were paid by the smile.

Nick said, "I'd better help him. Bert's Italian is— primitive."

"So's his English," I muttered to his retreating back.

"So are we going or not?" Nancy asked.

"Not."

"Honestly, Lana. Why did we *come* on this trip if you don't plan to have any *fun*? We agreed we'd do everything interesting that came up." But the only thing she considered interesting was going out with strange men, and now with Bert Garr.

"I didn't come to meet up with that creep of a Bert Garr. Contessa Linguini!"

"You're so judgmental! It's a natural mistake. I think we should accept."

It had been a grave mistake to come on this trip with Nancy. I should have believed all the magazine articles that told me women could travel alone. "You suit yourself. I'm going back to the hotel."

CHAPTER 2

For the next five minutes Nancy and I argued out the pros and cons of the date. "It'll be fun," she urged. "We wanted to have some glamour and romance. Nick's a dream, and I'll be with Bert."

That was her ace. The joker in the deck was, would Nick like me? A Nick devouring Nancy with his eyes didn't promise me much fun. A Nancy sulking for the next week was even less appealing, since we shared a room. We continued walking around, looking at the paintings, but half our attention was on the doorway and the beautiful Contessa, and in my case, Nick Hansen.

"This is the real Italy," Nancy said. "Just look at the people. Isn't this better than our tour, with old Ivor complaining about his bile, and that Miss Jamieson that wrote a book about Italy a zillion years ago always correcting the guides about everything?"

"But then there's Ron Evereton," I reminded her. Our tour guide was no match for Nick, but he left Bert far behind.

"He'll still be there tomorrow."

I had saved for three years for this trip. My grandiose plan of going unescorted through Europe had eventually dwindled to the tour package, and last Christmas, Nancy decided she'd come, too. We were too inexperienced to tackle the exchange of monies, the reservations, the awful mountain of luggage that would accompany Nancy. Her cup

Ż bras alone would fill a suitcase. Clothes were her passion. At school, she often changed at lunch hour, although she wore a smock over her dress. She had smocks in five pastel shades, one for each day of the week.

Our trip had been broadening and educational, but no magic had seeped in. Meeting Bert and coming to this art show were the first unusual things that had happened, unless you could call getting lost on the Paris subway unusual. Maybe I was too hidebound. You had to give life a little push once in awhile, or at least not dig in your heels and resist fate. "All right," I agreed. "We'll go out with them, but remember *you* have the pleasure of fighting with Rome's telephone system to notify the group."

"We'll go to the hotel and change instead," she suggested. "I should explain to Ron in person."

Considering the state of our hair and clothes and my toe, this wasn't a bad idea. We strolled through the crowd, listening to the Babel of foreign voices that still thrilled me after two weeks in Europe. The rough gutturals of German erupted incongruously from a pretty young girl. A Japanese couple conversed apologetically in light, staccato bursts. The throng moved about. Behind me, a man was speaking French. This sounded less strange after just being in France. French was my minor at college, but I still couldn't understand every word. They don't often use the phrases found in textbooks. I turned around, and noticed the Frenchman was speaking to the Contessa, detached from Bert and Nick now. She answered in flawless French. The Frenchman was uninteresting. He was small, middle-aged, and his nose was a little askew.

Nancy got lost in the crowd. I looked around and saw her just walking away from Bert and Nick. She'd probably told them we had accepted. I began working my way toward them, concealed by the throng. "It's agreed then, you take Lana Morton off my hands," I heard Bert say.

"But she's so tall, and so bad-tempered!" Nick objected, in the peevish way of a child objecting to wearing galoshes.

"You can sweet-talk her, you old Casanova, you," Bert laughed. "I owe you one, buddy."

"A very large one."

My heart shriveled. I wanted to run and hide my head in a corner, but I stayed riveted to the spot while they continued talking.

"*Signore* to *signore*, isn't that Nancy something?" Bert asked.

Bert, the traitor, spotted me and came forward smiling. Nick followed, sizing me up as his evening's entertainment. I read the familiar, assessing, tentative look, tinged with resignation, and my shriveled heart swelled with self-righteous indignation. Let the sweet-talker try his line on me and I'd reduce him to a pulp.

"Lana," Bert said, grabbing my shoulder. I wrenched away and glared. "Here's the setup. We're all going to Nick's villa for a drink. Nance will phone the hotel from there and let them know you two are going AWOL on tonight's activities. We drive you to your hotel to change into your gladdest rags, and we all hit the town. Have dinner, then we take you for a quick peek at the Forum. Does it work for you?" He leaned forward and said out of the side of his mouth, "You've got to get a load of this dude's villa. *La dolce vita*, Italian style. Ain't nothing like it in Troy."

Over his shoulder, Nick attempted a seductive Latin smile. "If that's what you've all decided, I won't spoil your fun," I said, with as much disinterest as humanly possible. "Nancy is so eager."

"You won't regret it, and that's a promise."

"You shouldn't make promises you can't keep, Bert," I told him.

"Want to meet a real contessa?" he offered, to appease me. He looked around for the trophy. Her gray linen back was just gliding out the door. "Oh, she's gone. She'll be back. Can't make up her mind between the gray pic and the one with sheep."

I looked to see how Nick liked these descriptions of his paintings. I expected to see an ironic smile curve his lips. His dark eyes were lit with conspiratorial laughter. My anger stopped growing. It didn't shrink, but it didn't grow.

"They're all too expensive for me," I said, meaning to imply they were grossly over-priced.

"Hey, no freebies," Bert laughed, and lifted an arm to beckon Nancy forward. "Quitting time," he said. "I'll tell Alberto to keep an eye on things here, and lock up the store later. Where's the Alfa-Romeo parked, Nick?" His tongue caressed the car's name lovingly. Bert enjoyed having this bit of glory to show off to me and Nancy. "Luckily, Nick has a two plus two," he explained.

"Two plus two what?" Nancy asked.

"A double-seater."

"I'll bring the car around to the front," Nick offered.

We went out a side door and waited at the curb. Before too long there was a wheeze and clank, and a little sports car that had once been red, but was now mostly rusty dints, bumped to a stop in front of us. The front bumper was held on by baling wire. One windshield wiper sat at an irregular angle in the middle of the window, unmoving. Dreams of the villa faded to a hovel in one of those blind alleys. Nancy leaned close and said, "Uh oh, better get Maaco." I didn't laugh.

When I tried to open the door, it didn't move. Nick reached across and gave it a punch with the side of his fist.

"It sticks a bit in the heat," he said, smiling. Handy for torrid Rome.

"Did you have an accident?" Nancy asked.

"People are terrible drivers here," he explained.

I pushed the magazines and empty pop cans to the floor to make a space to sit down and said, "They're litter bugs, too, I see."

I'm a neat freak. I not only keep my pens and pencils in separate mugs on my desk, I also have a cutlery tray in my drawer to keep the paper clips from seducing the elastic bands. I keep my shoes on shoe racks, and my pantyhose in little padded bags, with the summer ones in a separate bag from the winter ones.

The surprising thing was that beneath the clutter, the interior of the car looked almost new. "Traffic's very hard on cars in Rome," Nick explained vaguely.

Bert and Nancy were soon settled in the backseat. I didn't think it was wise to try to seek verbal revenge during the death-defying business of driving in Rome. Nick clenched his jaw, leaned into the windshield, gripping the steering wheel with white knuckled hands, and, after a few hair-raising close calls, we pulled free of the lethal traffic of the Corso. He was heading up one of the hills of Rome, past the Porta del Popolo. Beyond an avenue of trees—not the phalliclike cypresses but a fuller sort—was an occasional glimmer of water, which Bert told us was the Tiber river. The houses looked like a set of ancient golden building blocks set close together. Many of them had red tiled roofs.

Nick pulled into a driveway at one of the houses and squealed to a stop, avoiding by millimeters a motorcycle that was chained to a pillar. "This is it," Bert announced. "What'd I tell you, ladies? Babylon on the Tiber. There's a terrace out back. You can catch the breeze, and from the side you can see the river."

Nick leaned his head close to mine, black liquid eyes gleaming. "Did you bring your binoculars?" He grinned, and got out to hold the door.

I smiled coolly. "My eyes work fine. So do my ears," I added menacingly. I saw a question grow on Nick's mobile face.

The house looked plain from the outside, and, of course, old. So much of Italy is crumbling to dust. The building had the consistency of a crumbcake. I felt if I touched it, chunks would fall off in my hand. But inside it was a charming blend of America and Europe, and not nearly as messy as the car, and much cooler. Persian rugs partially covered the tiled floor. On the whitewashed walls hung an assortment of art, some modern, some old. A weathered marble head of an ancient Roman sat on a chunk of Doric column in one corner. A palm tree at the window cast interesting shadows. The sofa was beige leather, low, squashy, piled with bright cushions which I itched to plump up and straighten out. An irregular-shaped piece of glass on a hunk of marble was the coffee table. A welter of magazines and a big pottery ashtray gave the place what is called a comfortable, lived-in

look by decorating magazines and non-compulsive person-
alities.

"Air-conditioning, what a relief," Bert said.

I was peering around this way and that, seeing what I
could take exception to, and spotted a blind flapping in the
kitchen. "Why are the windows open then?" I asked.

Nick shook his head in frustration. "My cleaning lady has
a cat. She lets it sit on the windowsill. I've told her to close
the window after."

The place didn't look newly cleaned. I wondered if Nick
shared Bert's penchant for exaggerating his style of living.
He went and closed the window. Nancy made the phone call
and when she came back, Bert asked, "What's your poison,
ladies?"

"Campari and soda," Nancy said.

"Ditto for you, Lana?"

I nodded. "Can we freshen up first?"

"Surely. There's a john just down the hall. In the upstairs
one there's a bidet." Show-off.

"Downstairs'll be fine," I said, and Nancy and I made a
quick trip to brush our hair and fix our lipstick.

"What do you think of the place?" Nancy asked, smiling
widely.

"Nice."

"Imagine, Nick has a whole house. Bert says they're
practically impossible to find—and cost a fortune, like New
York. And he owns it. His mother's Italian. She's divorced
from Nick's dad. He's American."

"Nick must get his looks from his mother."

"I don't know, he was raised by his dad, in the States."

"You've been with Bert too long already. You inherit
your looks, whoever raises you has no bearing on them.
What does he do—the father, I mean?"

"He has an electronics company, not computers. He does
defense stuff for the American government."

"Oh, one of those guys who sells nuts and bolts for a
couple of thousand dollars."

"Now don't start running Nick down, Lana. He likes
you," she said earnestly, in the interest of peace.

She began rooting in her rat's nest of a shoulder bag. "Can I borrow your pink lipstick? Now that I'm getting a tan, it looks better than my red." She went to the mirror, talking over her shoulder, "God, I hope I don't get skin cancer. I'm going to buy a sun hat tomorrow." Hers had blown out a bus window two days ago.

We hastily fixed our faces and met Nick just coming into the hall with a tray of drinks. There was a bottle of Campari and a soda siphon on the tray. Bert was behind him, carrying another tray with glasses and an ice bucket. On the terrace there were padded lounge chairs and a glass-topped table. It was nice and cool, shaded by the house, with clipped yews forming a privacy hedge. Nothing a scorned lady could take sane exception to.

"Sit here," Nick suggested, indicating a pair of chairs a little removed from the table where Nancy and Bert were settling in. "This is the view of the Tiber."

I stared into the dense hedge. "I thought it'd be wet."

"If you stand on your tiptoes and squint, you catch an occasional glint of green. That's it."

The more interesting view was the sprawl of Rome, its domes and towers and campaniles gilded by the setting sun, with the stream of traffic just below us. A lovely cool breeze blew in. "They call it the *ponentino*—the westerly," Nick explained. "It comes from the sea."

We sat down edgily to become acquainted. He said "Cheers!" and clinked his glass against mine. We drank. I wondered why I had asked for Campari. A nice tall Tom Collins would have been better, but the alcohol had a soothing effect. I decided to forget that Nick and I were both here under duress and try to enjoy myself.

In fact Nick looked so handsome in that romantic setting that I readied myself to be fascinating. But before I could speak, he looked me dead in the eye and said, "I expect I should apologize for abetting Bert. You didn't want to come, did you, Lana?"

"No more than you did."

"I was eager to come," he lied glibly.

"So I gathered from your general air of reluctance."

"All right, I had made other plans. It doesn't mean we can't be civilized about it. You're a very handsome woman."

"And you're a pretty man," I retaliated.

Nick looked confused, sensing it wasn't a compliment, but not knowing how to object. "Bert twisted my arm. He's crazy about your friend," he said.

"She's my cousin, actually."

"Oh really? He didn't say so. You're so different from each other." Before I could fully interpret this insult, he continued. "He's often told me about her—their broken engagement. That's why he left Troy, you know, because of the family's opposition to the marriage."

Bert hadn't changed. Still inventing intrigues. I opened my lips to correct this lie, and closed them again. Why dump on Bert? Nancy and I would only be here for one evening. Bert had to spend the rest of his life here, and if he had made a friend in Nick, what good would it do for me to expose him? "I didn't know that," I replied.

"Oh yes. I hope, for his sake, that he can patch it up."

"He'll have to move fast. We'll be leaving Rome tonight."

"Life can't be planned in too much detail. I always leave room for happy accidents—like spending some time with you," he added, with a certain unconvincing continental charm.

"And having your arm twisted into taking me to dinner," I murmured, while my mind rapidly analyzed his speech. Was he hinting that we should remain longer in Rome? I knew he expected the conversation to become a flirtation, but I had no intention of obliging him. "It was quite a coincidence, meeting Bert. I haven't seen him since high school. It must be—oh, eight years."

Something in Nick's eyes told me he understood my change of topic, and was willing to go along with it. "I usually meet an old friend when I travel. In Paris I met my kindergarten teacher at the top of the Eiffel Tower. She didn't recognize me, of course, but I spotted her." His accent was beguiling. It wasn't the honking New England sound. Italy had softened it, blurring the vowels, fuzzing the endings.

"That's true, about meeting people in strange places. I was browsing through Harrods and met my dentist." It was pleasant to speak nonchalantly about Paris and London. I felt worldly, cosmopolitan, sitting on a terrace in Rome with a beautiful man, who was trying to flirt with me.

"Teachers and dentists—odd we both met people we'd normally avoid."

He knew bloody well I was a teacher! "Well, dentists don't pull your teeth when you just meet them in a store, and I'll try not to teach you anything."

A little twitch of amusement moved Nick's lips. "Do you think you could?" he asked.

"Only you would know whether you're capable of learning."

"I can't if you don't even try."

"Where did you meet Bert?" I asked hastily, to cut short this ambiguous line of talk.

"I forgot you're a teacher. Honest."

I shrugged my shoulders to show no offense had been taken and repeated the question.

"I saved his life in a boating accident on the Tiber," Nick explained. "According to an old legend, that makes me responsible for him."

"And now he's your manager, or agent, or something?"

"Agent, and a damned good one. Bert's clever—a rough diamond. The gallery that exhibited me was taking thirty-five percent. Bert takes fifteen. Sales haven't fallen off since I went with him either. I was already becoming known a little. Bert felt I could get along without the sponsorship of an established gallery."

"Where does he sell your works then?"

"He puts on an annual exhibition, and of course I get commissions. It's a living," he said modestly.

"He mentioned you were in Paris . . ."

"Yes, when I graduated from art school in New York, I went to Paris to study for a year."

"Isn't the more innovative work being done in the States now?"

"It is, really, but the lure of the Left Bank drew me. Actually it was wasted time, but very enjoyably wasted time," he added, with a nostalgic look.

"Wine, women, and song, I suppose?"

"That, too, but mostly painting. I fell into an abstract expressionist period, under the influence of my teacher. Angry streaks of red and black and yellow and white. My French Frustration period, I call it. I had an agent there, but he didn't manage to sell anything. My money was running low. I took what I had left and ran—to Italy."

"Rome isn't cheap either."

"I went to Florence first, the banks of the Arno, the cradle of Renaissance art, and studied the Botticellis, the Leonardos, the Raphaels—what craftsmen. I realized it wasn't abstract art I wanted to do. I wanted to be a master craftsman, too."

"We saw the Botticellis at the Uffizi. They were magnificent."

"I used to practice drawing there. I'd sit for a whole day, sketching a hand, the setting of an eye, the fold of a garment. They can't really teach that at school. In the Rennaissance they had the right idea. You observe the masters, copy them, do it, and do it, and do it again till you're in control of your hand." He flexed his long, brown, artistic fingers, innocent of jewelry. He didn't even wear a watch.

"I'd say you have your hand under control now, Nick, to judge by your exhibition."

"For landscapes. The hard part is yet to come—the human form. The face—you have a Botticelli face, Lana." His dark eyes studied me closely. I never felt like one of those serene graces in my entire life.

"You use tempera, I think," I said, ignoring that comparison.

Nick's eyes glowed with passion as he talked about his art. "It's a son-of-a-gun," he said, shaking his head. "Bert says I'm a masochist. It's laborious, working in layers, preparing the materials. But it gives a smooth, luminous effect you can't get with oils."

"Is it true they use egg white?"

"Egg yolk, as a binder for the ground pigments. The yellow fades; it doesn't discolor the pigments. I'll show you my studio later. And how about you, Lana? That's a lovely name, by the way. So—gentle," he said, hesitating over the word. It sounded liquid on his tongue. "What is it you teach?"

"English."

He nodded. "In Troy. Bert's told me a little about Troy."

"I think he said you were raised in Boston?"

"Yes, by my father, nominally. I was sent to boarding school for most of the year. My parents divorced when I was eight. Dad met Mom here, in Rome, and married her. He was the Italian rep for an American electronics company at the time. They recalled him to the States. Mom tried to live in the States, but her heart was here, she said. Rome is called the city of big emotions. She found everything else in the States too big, and the emotions not big enough. They're both remarried now."

I found it strange he hadn't gone with his mother. "Do you see much of your mom?"

He shook his head forlornly. The continental charmer was replaced by a lost little boy. After all these years. "Her heart found a new home in Paris. I used to see her there. We visit."

I didn't like to ask too many questions. I saw a lot of those strangely disoriented children at school. From one-parent homes, from divorced homes, living with new fathers or mothers. You could tell when there was trouble at home. The kids become distracted, sometimes unruly. Would they become Casanovas when they grew up? My heart always went out to them. The word divorce was never mentioned between my mom and dad. We're an old-fashioned, stable family. One son, one daughter, lived in the same two-story brick house forever. Dad owns a drug store, Mom works there now sometimes, since the children are all grown up. Bob, my brother, is studying pharmacy at college. One day he'll take over the family store. Stable as the Rock of Gibraltar. I used to sense some glamour in my own 'divorced' friends when I was young. My life seemed dull compared to theirs.

I briefly described my family background to Nick. "That's marvelous," he said gently, almost enviously. "I'd like to have a family like that, one day."

I felt a little sorry for him. Everyone's glass became empty at the same time. "Another one for the road, folks?" Bert called.

"Maybe we should start making plans for dinner," Nancy suggested.

It was nice and peaceful on the terrace with the traffic streaming by below and the skyline of Rome gilded by the lowering sun, casting purple shadows on the house next door. And Nick wasn't so bad after all.

He looked a question at me. "We can eat here, if you like. It'll save time," he said.

"Whatever you like."

"We'll have another drink and discuss it," he decided. "Do you really want to drink Campari?"

"No."

"Bert, let's concoct a special Roman cocktail for the ladies."

"You're on. This Campari stuff is the pits."

Bert got up and they went into the house. I joined Nancy at the table. "Guess what," I said. She cocked an eyebrow. "Bert told Nick he used to be engaged to you. The family disapproved. He didn't say which family. Was it yours, or his?" I asked, with a conspiratorial grin.

She met my gaze coolly. "Actually we never told our families."

"You mean you *were* engaged to him!"

"Secretly—for two weeks. It was Bert's last year of high school. He wanted us to run away. You know I always wanted a big wedding. I wanted to wait a year till I finished high school. That's why we broke up—because I wouldn't marry him right away."

I was shocked into disbelief. "Good lord!"

"And don't you dare tell anyone at home!"

We sat silently a minute while I digested this. "Why?" was all I could think of to say.

"We had our reasons. And I wasn't pregnant! We never—you know. I'd rather not talk about it right now." She flopped her blond mane over her shoulder and looked nobly into the yew hedge.

"All right," I agreed, but I meant to get the whole story soon. "Nick suggested we could eat here. What do you think?"

"Who does the cooking? Or does he have a cook?"

"I don't know. He probably has a woman who cooks and cleans."

In a few minutes the men came back, carrying four tall glasses, filled with a pink fizzy liquid and a lot of ice cubes. "What's in this?" Nancy asked.

"Ask not for whom the bell tolls," Bert replied.

"It sounds lethal," she said with a laugh.

Bert looked confused. "It'll curl your hair," he promised, and took a sip. "Not bad, if I do say so myself."

It was better than not bad. It was delicious. I could detect a variety of fruit juices below the gin. Pineapple, orange, lemon, and probably cranberry to color it. Nick and I stayed at the table and we all talked, the conversation becoming noisier and sillier as we drank. The Roman cocktails were strong, and on an empty stomach they began to lend a hazy glow to the world. When our glasses were empty, Bert suggested another.

"Then we'll have to eat here," Nick said. "I couldn't drive after another of these bombs."

"You can't drive anyway," Bert said, with a bleary, laughing eye. "Creamed his new car the week he got it. Has an accident a week. Worst driver I ever saw, and that's saying plenty."

"I'm an excellent driver," Nick said with haughty indifference. "It's just that other drivers keep getting in my way."

"Selfish bastards, wanting a piece of your road." Bert grinned.

They took the glasses in. "I'm getting powerful hungry," Nancy said, perhaps because she saw the gleam of curiosity in my eyes, and still didn't want to talk about her engagement. "I wonder if the cook's making dinner yet."

"It's not even seven o'clock."

She got up and went peering in windows. "They're coming back," she said. "Oh great, there's a little guy going into the kitchen now. Nick has a male servant. Classy, huh?"

She was innocently sitting at the table when the men came out with our refills. After half a glass, Bert said, "Let's go swimming."

"Where?" I asked.

"Hell, there's a river just down there. Here it comes, the girls don't have bathing suits. I bet you've never gone skinny-dipping with a guy, have you, Lana?"

I have never even been skinny-dipping with girls. "Lots of times," I said.

"Then let's swim."

"I'm too tired. I'd drown."

"Not to worry. Nick'll save you. I ever tell you about how Nick and I met? I was in a little rowboat with a chick—Gina her name was. I tried to get friendly and she pushed me overboard." Everybody laughed. "Seriously! I can't swim a stroke. I was floundering like a fish out of—in water and who should come along but old Nick. The devil himself. Fished me out, brought me up here. Been buddies ever since, right, buddy?"

Nick gave a lopsided grin. I suspect all our grins were growing pretty lopsided. How else could it happen that we fell fast asleep, sitting in our chairs, with our heads inching ever closer to the table for support? I remember the conversation petering out, and Nick's black eyes growing fuzzy. I vaguely recall Nancy saying, "I'm starved. When do we eat?"

The next thing I remember is Bert shaking my arm. "Wow!" he exclaimed. "Hangover city! Nick must have slipped a mickey in that drink. My head feels like Mount Helena. Thar she blows!"

It was dark. Below, the stream of cars had turned to ribbons of light, piercing the blackness. The soft night air felt refreshingly cool against my fevered brow. I shook myself to attention. "Good lord, what time is it? Our bus to Naples leaves at ten."

"You've missed the boat, kiddo. It's ten-o-five."

CHAPTER 3

"Great, we've missed our bus. How are we going to get to Naples? There must be a public bus or something." I jiggled Nancy's elbow till she woke up.

"Huh?" She looked all around, dazed and frowning. "Where are we?"

"If it's Wednesday, it must be Rome," Bert told her. "Roma, Nance. Ring any bells? Art exhibit, Nick Hansen. Me, li'l ol Bert Garr."

"What—Bert?" She shook the sleep from her big green eyes. As sense returned she jumped up in alarm. "What time is it?"

"Ten-o-five," Bert said.

"That's impossible!" We all exchanged a confused look. It *did* seem incredible that all four of us could have conked out.

"Not to worry," Bert said. "I'll get you to Naples by morning to meet up with your tour. Thing is, you won't be able to book a hotel room in Rome tonight. All the hotels are booked up tight as a drum at the height of the season."

The look Nancy and I exchanged held a tacit question. Did that wretch of a Bert plan this? Had he doctored our drinks, or something? It seemed suspicious that he was the first to wake up. My head felt woolier than a sheepskin, and a lot more confused than a couple of drinks should have made it.

Bert walked over and shook Nick. "A bit of a problemo

30

has come up, Nick. We all goofed off, and the ladies have missed their bus to Naples. Boy, what a cocktail hour that was."

Nick stirred to life by slow degrees. First he quit snoring, then his eyelids fluttered open, then he lifted his head, yawned, saw me staring at him, and frowned. "What happened? Christ, it's dark! What time is it?" He leapt up from his chair, graceful even in that explosive action.

"Ten-o-five," Bert said again.

"It can't be!"

"Seeing is believing," Bert told him, and pointed at his knockoff Gucci, which was of course invisible in the shadows.

We all discussed sheepishly how this bizarre thing had happened. Both Nancy and I had been dead tired from travel fatigue. It had been hot, and we were hungry, and we'd had all those drinks. Still, I was surprised that two healthy young men had keeled over so easily. My surprise held a tinge of incredulity. Had Bert pulled off one of his stunts to keep Nancy in Rome longer? I had suspected some scheme when Nick spoke of life not being planned in too much detail. Of equal importance to me, had Nick aided and abetted him? Nick's surprise upon awaking seemed genuine. He had even been snoring a little.

"We'll have to drive you to Naples," Nick said.

"On an empty stomach?" Bert asked. It was a matter of growing concern to us all.

"How come your cook didn't wake us?" Nancy asked.

Nick looked blank. "Cook? I don't have a cook. My cleaning lady will cook, but I have to arrange it in advance."

"Lady? I saw a man in your kitchen."

"That was the cocktails talking," Bert said with a laugh. "I was seeing a few pink elephants myself. Whoa, major hangover! D.T.'s, here I come."

"I saw a man," Nancy insisted.

The men exchanged a questioning look. A *meaningful,* questioning look. It was just a quick glance, but I caught a fleeting glimpse of fear in Bert's expression. "What did he look like?" he asked, trying to sound nonchalant.

"He was a little, dark-haired man," she said.

He relaxed visibly. In fact, he laughed aloud in relief.

"Who do you think it was, Bert? The man who was chasing you this afternoon?" I asked firmly. No hint of uncertainty clouded my voice.

"There was nobody chasing me this afternoon. I don't know what you're talking about. And there was no man in the kitchen. Don't forget it was after the Camparis and the Roman cocktails that Nancy 'saw' this apparition."

Nancy rubbed her forehead. "Maybe it was just a shadow. Well, if we're going to eat, let's get going."

"I thought we were eating here," Bert said. "Nick's a world-class chef."

And he didn't want to leave the house. Was that it? Was somebody after Bert—or maybe Bert and Nick? It was Nick's house where Nancy saw the man. They had both looked startled and rather knowing when Nancy dropped her little bombshell. I studied Bert closely. Whatever had upset him, he'd gotten over it now. He seemed perfectly relaxed. Maybe I was imagining things. I had no love for Bert, and was quick to accuse. The poor guy was probably just short of money. Nancy wasn't sure she'd seen a man, and I hadn't actually seen anyone following him.

"I have all kinds of cold meats and cheese—bread," Nick offered vaguely.

"Let's chow down. I'm so hungry my chest is caving in," Bert said, and we trouped into the house.

It was a charming old kitchen, with a white tiled counter and blue flowered tiles rising up to the cupboards. Nick got out a tray of spicy cold cuts: mortadella sliced paper thin, dotted with black peppers; pale pink prosciutto; darker salamis. The tantalizing fumes of garlic and smoked meat filled the air. Next he brought out cheeses: blue-veined Gorgonzola; a piquant Asiago; a soft cheese that looked like Gruyère, but was called Groviera. I sliced a long loaf of crusty bread. Nancy and Bert set the table in the kitchen. Everything seemed perfectly normal, even cozy.

"Vino would hit the spot with this feast. A hair of the dog," Bert said. He received three baleful glares. "Right, I'll put on some water for coffee."

The makeshift meal of cold meats piled high on bread tasted better than haute cuisine. "Hunger is the best sauce," Nancy said, reaching for the meat tray. The rest of us were too ravenous for much conversation.

"We need vitamins. Some melons and green grapes would help," Nick decided, and brought a bowl of fruit to the table.

"This is fun!" I exclaimed. "I'm kind of glad we all fell asleep."

"Even if it interrupts your schedule?" Nick asked archly.

"Schedules are for trains," Bert scoffed. "Boy, was I fed up with schedules when I was touring. You can take your schedules and stick 'em where the sun don't shine."

"We're scheduled all day by bells at school. It's the unplanned things that make travelling so enjoyable," Nancy said. Her look said that if I'd had my way, we would have missed this adventure.

"You're right," Bert agreed. "You know what would be slightly terrific, if I do say so myself? Why don't you gals stick around Rome for a few days, catch up with the tour in Naples the day after tomorrow? You'd still have a morning there to see the bay."

At last it was out in the open. I slid a surreptitious look at Nick, and caught him watching me with interest. He smiled. I stiffened. "Good idea," he said, just as I exclaimed, "That's impossible!"

"Oh, Lana!" Nancy said angrily.

The three of them started persuading me. "We just agreed it's the unplanned things that are fun," Nancy pointed out. Bert assured me Naples was so insignificant it was often left out of the tours entirely. You'd almost wonder why it was on the maps.

Nick added his mite. "I wanted to show you my studio, Lana. We'll do some sightseeing in the afternoon—you haven't toured the Forum. You can't leave Rome without seeing it. We'll drive you and Nancy to Naples for dinner. You can sleep here."

I leapt from my chair, much less gracefully than Nick had done earlier. "Sleep here?"

"I have four bedrooms," he assured me earnestly. A quick eye movement to Bert and Nancy, followed by a concentrated stare told me he was working to bring about a reconciliation between Romeo and Juliet. "It seems a shame for you old friends not to have a day together at least. You'll want to talk about old times."

"Let's stay," Nancy urged. "Nick has four bedrooms, Lana," she repeated, quite unnecessarily.

"Four? Hell, we only need two," Bert said. He received two more baleful glares, and a curious look from Nick, not entirely devoid of interest. "What did I say? We're all consenting adults, right? Don't worry, ladies. No diseases here. Right, Nick?" Nick scowled at him. "Well, anyway, you might as well spend the night. It'll save driving to Naples in the dark."

"We'll have to get our things from the hotel," I mentioned. My maidenly show of reluctance had been made. I didn't really feel like driving all the way to Naples in the dark. I felt weary, and hung over. There was no guarantee we could find a hotel room, and if we had to stay in Rome, a free night's lodging would be appreciated.

"The hotel will have packed your bags," Bert said.

"I can drive you over now and pick them up," Nick offered.

"That seems like a lot of trouble." Even getting up from the table seemed a terrible imposition on my body.

"I don't mind, but maybe you should come over with me," Nick suggested. "I doubt if they'd hand them over to me."

Going with Nick lent resilience to my tired body. "All right."

"That means Nance and me get stuck with cleaning up, right?" Bert asked.

I just smiled.

It was exciting, gliding down the hill with Nick in his

sporty red junk-heap of a car. Rome's panoply of lights, spread below, hinted at nocturnal gaiety. I was with a handsome, fascinating stranger. This was what the trip was all about, really. Not just dusty museums, bleeding toes, and a confusing jumble of churches. I knew that tonight, despite its problems, would stand out in memory as the culmination of my trip. But I didn't lose my head completely. I took advantage of the opportunity to quiz Nick.

"Who do you think that was prowling in your kitchen, Nick? I saw the look you and Bert exchanged."

He shrugged his shoulders. "It's nothing to worry about. Just an angry boyfriend."

"Which one of you's been fooling around with a married woman?"

"Bert, and I said boyfriend. She's only engaged."

"Are you sure it was Bert? It was your kitchen he was in."

"*You* were in my kitchen too, Lana. I don't have to remind you there was no fooling around. Forget the questions and just enjoy Roma. Have you noticed, Roma spelled backwards is amor, the biggest emotion of them all."

"And La Roma backwards is amoral."

He lifted his eyes from the wheel long enough to glare in frustration. "You're the only woman in the world who would think of that! Don't you ever just relax and enjoy your life? You're so uptight."

"And tenacious. Who was the man?"

He growled something, doubtlessly profane, in Italian. "Bert has an idea the boyfriend's following him. He's probably right, and the boyfriend followed him to my house. But I hope you don't tell Nancy. Naturally, he doesn't want her to know. The affair's all over now. How do you think it's going with them—Bert and your cousin?"

"All right, I guess, but we'll be leaving tomorrow."

He turned his head and smiled at me in the darkness. "Sure I can't persuade you to stay a little longer?"

"Quite sure."

"I could be *very* persuasive, if you'd give me half a chance." He reached for my hand.

I moved it away. Little did he know how stubborn I could be. "Try and see if you can persuade your car to stay off the curb." We missed a lamppost by inches.

Feminine heads turned when we went into the hotel. Nick didn't even notice. He actually didn't know how gorgeous he was. I took his arm possessively, cherishing every jealous glance.

The rooms were already paid for by the tour company. Nick did the necessary talking in Italian, I produced my passport as verification that I was me. We got the bags and went back to Nick's villa. I thought he might park along the way and try his hand at persuasion, but he didn't even try, and I was a little disappointed. He was just being flirtatious so I'd stay and let Bert have his chance with Nancy. It was midnight when we got back. In spite of our unexpected snooze and the coffee, we were all dog tired.

The bedroom that Nick showed me had a key in the lock, a big double bed with a feather tick and a bleached cotton duvet, a dark, carved dresser, and an old gilt mirror. It was charming. "Why don't we share this room?" Nancy suggested. I interpreted this to mean that she wanted to be safe from Bert and agreed.

"There's a bathroom en suite," Nick said, nodding to a door.

He said good night, we said thank you, he left, and I locked the door.

The bathroom had a shower, a new one that worked. I showered first, ostensibly to allow myself time to doctor my toe afterward while Nancy had her shower. My real motive was to get in before she made a mess of the room. One of the little unexpected annoyances of the trip was that Nancy, who turns out looking as neat as a pin, leaves chaos behind. She soon came out, wrapped in a big white towel and pulled the shower cap off, fluffing up her mane in the mirror.

"I'm sure I saw a man in the kitchen earlier," she said.

I thought of Bert and the other woman, and I thought of

Nick's request that I keep quiet about it. "Maybe it was a neighbor, or something."

"Yeah." She began rubbing cream on her face.

"Did Bert give you a hard time while we were gone, or why did you decide to share my room?"

She looked annoyed at the question. "Of course not. Bert's a gentleman, even if he is . . . It was just that comment about only needing two rooms—it put me off a little."

"Do you want to talk about that engagement now?"

"No. Bert looked good tonight, didn't he?" she said in a musing way. "It's all the weight he's lost. He works out now."

I listened, trying to comprehend her fondness for Bert. "Maybe if I put another Band-Aid on top of this first one, making a cross . . ." Was I just being a snob about Bert? The collection of clichés and last year's buzz words he called conversation appalled my English teacher's soul. They were kind of pathetic really. He was like a verbal magpie, picking up tawdry tinsel adornments to enliven his speech, in an effort for approval. *Wanting* to please should count for something.

Nancy put on her nighttime brassiere. She has some in a size larger than she wears for daytime, to keep her ample bosoms in form. She shimmied into her nightie, yawning. "I'd like to see Nick's studio tomorrow, too. I'm curious about the tempera technique."

I found myself yawning, too, and rolled over on my back to examine the crossed Band-Aids. "I hope I don't get an infection in this darned blister. Tomorrow I'm wearing sneakers."

"I told you to."

We were asleep almost before our heads touched the pillows. When I awoke, it was daylight and the other side of the bed was empty. Nancy was an early bird. Not bothering to pick her nightie off the floor or wipe her hairs out of the sink saved her a little time, too. I had an uneasy feeling she was downstairs making headway with Nick in the studio, and scrambled into a sundress to join them. I did her wrong.

She was with Bert in the living room, eating bread and figs and drinking coffee, while they nursed their hangovers. I felt like a dishrag myself.

"Where's Nick?" I asked.

"In his studio. Bert's going to his office to contact people who left their names at the gallery. He's getting together a retrospective show for Nick, too," Nancy explained.

"He's kind of young for that, isn't he?"

"The boy's making a bit of a ripple in the art world now—we're talking tidal wave," Bert said. "The Contessa wanted to see some of his earlier stuff. It'll bring a better price if the lady has some competition, so I'm going to put together a retrospective show."

"That's clever, Bert," I said unthinkingly. His chest swelled, and he smiled beatifically. I couldn't remember ever complimenting Bert before.

"All in a day's work," he said, and began talking about his P.R. business in a self-congratulatory way.

After breakfast, we went to Nick's studio. Bert came to the door with us and called, "I'm off now, Nick."

"Take care," Nick called. They exchanged a peculiar look. Not a warning, exactly, but there was something strange, or secretive, in it. I ascribed it to the angry boyfriend. Nancy, who was more interested in the studio, didn't see it.

She was a step ahead of me into the studio, so I hastened to her side. It was a large, square, austere room, well lit, and neat as a pin. At least Nick was a stickler about the cleanliness of his work space. On the easel there was a canvas with a picture partially sketched in. This one was of a person, an old man standing in the doorway of a mountain house. He was shading his eyes with his gnarled hand. A dog sat at his feet, gazing up at him.

Nick was at a table, looking very continental and bohemian in a shirt the color of the Italian sky on a summer day. Like the rest of us, he was showing some signs of being hung over. The purple smudges under his eyes gave him an interesting air of dissipation. He was breaking an egg to show us how he mixed the tempera.

"I break these and dry all the white off the yolk before mixing," he explained. "You can buy a commercial binder now, but I do it the old way. It gives a tough, permanent film." He broke the yolk sack and mixed up the yolk in a little dish, unscrewed a cap from a bottle of vermilion powder, mixed the powder with the yolk, and applied it to paper with a red sable watercolor brush. I know these details about the brush as Nancy asked a good many questions.

"I didn't realize you painted on paper," she exclaimed.

"Actually I paint on wood, but this'll give the idea. It dries quickly, and you can apply more coats to get the shade you want."

Nancy made noises of interest, and spoke of luminosity and opaque touches. Nick talked about emulsions, and oily and colloidal ingredients for quite a while. The most interesting thing I learned is that hens' eggs contain oil in the yolks. When we had both dabbed the tempera mixture on paper, we looked around at other items.

"Are these your cartoons?" Nancy asked. "Not as in Mickey Mouse," she explained to me. "They call the preliminary sketches for paintings 'cartoons'."

I bristled at her condescending tone. As if anyone could get through the Louvre and the Uffizi Gallery without knowing that! "I was wondering why there were no balloons with words coming out of their mouths." We went to the far side of the table, where there was a litter of drawings. I recognized the old man's face, his hand, the dog.

"I hear Bert's preparing a retrospective show," I said.

Nick nodded. "It's a bit premature, but no harm in thinking big. Some clients have shown interest in my French Frustration period."

"Can we see some of your older expressionist paintings?" Nancy asked.

"Sure, if Bert can find them. I had a couple around here someplace, but they're missing. Bert's taking a look at his place. I left most of them in Paris with my old agent, Boisvert. He was supposed to forward me the money if he sold any. Since he didn't, I'll ask him to send the paintings along, if he hasn't thrown them out. It's been five years."

They talked some more about his tempera paintings. Nancy was interested in the laborious method of deciding on the organization of the painting, doing the cartoons, transferring them to the wood and the troubles encountered with the medium, which sounded like a whole saga in itself. After half an hour, I had learned more about tempera than I really wanted to know and asked, "How long will Bert be gone? Does he live far away?"

"He lives in the Subura, just above the Colosseum, but he took my motorcycle. He should be back any minute," Nick said. He glanced at my watch and frowned. I wondered if the irate boyfriend had caught up with Bert. It's funny how worrying about someone can make you like him. I was worried that Bert might be beaten up, lying helpless in one of those cobblestone alleys.

"Let's have another cup of that coffee," Nancy suggested. "I still feel lousy. What was in those cocktails, Nick?"

"Just gin and fruit juices and soda water." He wore a puzzled frown, and I knew what he was thinking. A couple of gins, even on top of the Campari, shouldn't have knocked us all for a loop. "Am I imagining things, Nancy, or did you say you saw a dark-haired man in my kitchen last night?"

"I thought I did."

I had the feeling Nick didn't want to alarm us, but I also felt he was becoming alarmed himself. "Are you sure he wasn't a big guy, blond hair, square jaw?"

"No, he was a small, dark-haired man. Why?"

He shrugged. "Nothing."

Concern for Bert began to burn at my vitals. We went back into the living room. Nick couldn't sit still. He kept asking me what time it was, pacing, going to the window every few minutes to look for Bert. "I'm going to give Bert a call," he finally said, and left the room. The phone, a red modern-looking one, was in his studio.

When he came back about three minutes later, his

concern had es
I felt little rippl
answer. I think I sh

"Why? What's the r

"Probably nothing, but

"What are we waiting for

"There *is* something wrong!

We grabbed up our purses, Ni
keys, and we were off in the little rea
clanking, windshield wiper disturbing
drove, Nick invented a ridiculous sto
wanting to talk to Bert about a business misu anding,
and I sat worrying my conscience, wondering whether I
shouldn't tell Nancy the truth.

We coasted about half the way down the hill into Rome,
made a turn, and went through streets that became narrower
and shabbier and bumpier as we progressed. There was one
benefit—the windshield wiper fell back down to the bottom
of the window. We hurtled past dun-colored houses, small
stores, and seedy restaurants, dodging children and cats.
There were no sidewalks, and the street was too narrow for
another car to pass safely. Since there was no room for
parking, Nick squealed the car to a stop right in front of the
door of a big old stone building with a magnificent carved
archway that was fast returning to its original quarried state.

The combination of grandeur and decay is one of the
things that stands out in my mind about Rome. A doorway
or arch or statue that belongs in a castle will suddenly pop
up in the midst of decayed poverty. This building had been
converted into apartments.

"He has the flat on the second floor at the back," Nick
said. "I'll be right back."

"We'll all go," Nancy said.

"No!" His answer was sharp. "I—I'll go. No need for all
of us to go storming in."

Nick pushed the loose door open and bolted up the steps
three at a time. "There's something funny going on,"
Nancy said, sounding concerned. "Nick wouldn't be this
worried if some man just wants to talk to Bert."

_____," I said.

_____ wing on her thumb. "And he asked _____ blond guy. I mean, somebody like that could _____ stuffing out of Bert. You thought when we first saw Bert yesterday that he was kind of looking over his shoulder, didn't you?"

"Yes."

"He was walking so fast, as if he was trying to get away from somebody. This is all starting to smell fishy. I'm going to see if Bert's there. If he's all right."

"I'm not staying alone in an illegally parked car."

"Maybe you should, in case some of those kids steal the hubcaps."

"The car doesn't have any hubcaps. And I'm not staying in this slum alone. I'll probably be knifed in the back."

CHAPTER 4

We both went into the house, up the stairs, and down a dark corridor, which smelled of garlic and dust and sweat, to the apartment at the rear. "Imagine poor Bert, living here," Nancy said, with a shiver of distaste.

The apartment door was open. Nick stood in the middle of the room, looking around at a mess that went beyond giving me nervous spasms. It was just too much. A rust-colored sofa was pushed askew, a coffee table knocked over, a chair with the cushion thrown on the floor. At first I just thought Bert was an utter slob, which was, in fact, half the reason for the mess. Shoes in the middle of the floor, shirt thrown over a lamp, used glasses sitting all over—that was Bert's doing all right. But it didn't seem likely he had pushed his furniture all helter-skelter. I noticed there were copies of American magazines all over. *Time*, *People*, *Playboy*. This was how he kept in touch with home.

The air in the apartment smelled sour. "He's not here?" Nancy asked. Nick shook his head.

"Does he have an office?" I asked. "Didn't he say the pictures were at his office?"

"This is his office—he works out of his apartment," Nick told me.

"Oh." Of course. How like Bert to aggrandize the details of his living style.

"I'll check the bedroom. I can look out back and see if his car's gone," Nick said, and left.

43

Nancy began tidying the living room. I went the other way, toward what proved to be the kitchen. I discovered where the smell was coming from. A pitcher of milk had soured and curdled. A plate of butter had melted into a puddle, and there was a half a loaf of bread turning green on the counter. He hadn't been here for a week at least! But someone had been here, searching for something. I took the milk pitcher to the awful old tin sink and flushed it away. There was a magazine clipping taped above the sink. "The most difficult thing about becoming a millionaire is thinking you can do it." The clipping was splattered with grease and coffee grounds, and all curled up at the edges. He'd put it where he'd see it every day.

I felt like bawling for Bert. So ambitious, and so totally doomed to failure. He had the twentieth-century disease: he didn't want to do great things, he just wanted to be rich. The down-at-the-heels Gucci loafers, the knockoff watch—they were his little attempts at looking successful. Living a shabby life might be tolerable if you didn't have such high aspirations, but Bert had always wanted so badly to be "in" with the crowd. And in our day, money was the key. How proud he was of the Contessa, and the champagne and caviar, and how eager to brag to us about them.

When I returned to the living room, Nancy was in the hall, examining the door. "The door was kicked in," she pointed out. There were about one hundred years of kick marks on the outside, but the lock had been pulled off the door recently. The splinters looked raw. Nick came out of the bedroom. "His clothes are gone, but his car's still there," he said.

"What about your motorcycle?" I asked.

"No sign of it."

I showed him the state of the kitchen. "I don't think he's been here for days."

Instead of concern, Nick seemed slightly relieved. "Maybe he's all right then," he said. I gave him a questioning look. "It seems Bert's . . . moved," he explained.

"To get away from the large blond man who's been following him?" I asked.

"Was Luigi actually following him yesterday?"

"I think somebody was. You'd better tell Nancy the truth about Luigi."

He frowned and bit his lip. "Will it turn her off?"

"Why should it? She's been going out with men."

"Mind if we talk in the car? This place gives me the creeps."

I called a wild-eyed Nancy into the kitchen to tell her we were leaving. "I don't understand!" she said, close to tears. "Where is Bert? What's happened to him?"

"Nick's going to tell us shortly," I consoled her.

But once we were back in the car, Nick admitted he didn't have a clue where Bert was. We decided to head back to Nick's place since we didn't know where else to go, and since Bert might possibly have reached there safely. Nick said he could make a few phone calls and see if he could find out anything. In the meantime, he filled us in on what he *did* know.

"There's this girl," Nick said. "Maria's her name. Pretty, black hair, white skin. I don't know where Bert met her, but he went out with her a few times. He didn't know she was spoken for, but it seems she has a fiancé."

Nancy clammed up and crossed her arms, pretending to have lost interest. "Luigi's his name," I told her.

"Luigi—her fiancé—spoke to Bert rather sternly, I believe," Nick continued. "Since he's about seven feet tall, weighs close to three hundred pounds, and has a temper like Attila the Hun, I thought Bert would heed the warning."

"He would," Nancy said curtly.

I agreed. After four years of high school, you get to know a person, and Bert is not the kind of man to risk life and limb for a woman. He has a loud mouth, but he was also a Grade A chicken.

"And the reason he isn't in his apartment is that Luigi knows where he lives, and he's hiding somewhere?" I asked.

"That's the way I see it. I told him he could stay with me

when he first told me about Conan—Bert calls Luigi Conan. Bert said Conan knew he worked for me, and where I lived. It'd be the second place he'd look."

"And that's why you thought Conan might be at your house yesterday."

"It must have been some other woman's boyfriend," Nancy snipped from the backseat.

When Nick pulled into his driveway, the motorcycle was chained to a post. "He's back!" I exclaimed.

Nick and I went pelting in, with Nancy following behind, preparing to be cool with Bert.

A very pale, frightened Bert was pretending nothing unusual was going on. "You guys didn't tell me you were going out," he complained. "I didn't know if you'd taken the ladies on to Naples or what, Nick. Told you I'd only be a minute. Sorry, no sign of the old pix. Maybe you could paint up a few new ones in your old style. I really think Lingini might spring for one."

Nancy lifted her nose and sniffed. Then she sat on the sofa, picked up an art magazine, and began to riffle through it to show her total disinterest in Bert.

"Are you all right?" Nick asked Bert. I noticed then that Bert was rubbing his stomach and giving an occasional wince, although he wasn't wearing any visible bruises.

"Right as rain," he said, and gave a rictuslike smile.

"Where were you? When you didn't come back, we went to your apartment."

"Oh jeez, you didn't take the girls there! I should've told you, Nick. I moved. Couldn't stand the racket in that place. I'm subletting to a student. I thought it'd be fun to live in the Subura," he said, trying to put a good face on about his hovel. "It's the heart of old Rome. Most tourists don't even know it exists. Full of history. The street at the end used to go right to the Forum, but some old emperor carved it up. Still, it's a great location. How was my apartment?"

"He'd been there," Nick said. Bert gave a quelling look. "I told them about Luigi. You can't go on hiding it, Bert. When you disappeared, I had to give some explanation."

"Shit. Did he wreck everything? Is my stereo all right?"

"It's fine. The place was just disarranged," Nick assured him. "Where are you staying now?"

"I've taken a pensione by the week. That's where Conan got me this morning. I had a feeling he was following me yesterday, but I couldn't spot him."

"He got you!" Nancy flew up from the sofa, all concern. "Bert!"

He rubbed his stomach. "Guy's a pro. He kneads you like a wad of dough, and doesn't leave a sign. I retched myself sick."

"Oh Bert! Sit down. I'll get you some wine."

"Never mind the wine. A week in the hospital is what I need. Anybody know the symptoms of a ruptured spleen?" He tenderly rubbed his belly.

Nancy laid him down and lovingly tucked a cushion behind his head. He opened his shirt to reveal a mottled red torso. "We should have this brute arrested!" she said.

"Forget it. The guy'd have every punk in town after me. He's related to half of Rome. Boy, when Maria told me he was a librarian, I thought he'd be harmless. Huh, Conan the Librarian. He works at one of the art academies, cataloguing stuff. He could lift Grand Central Station with one hand."

"You should be a little more careful who you go out with," Nancy said primly.

"I wouldn't have gone out with her if you ever answered my letters."

I looked at Nancy. She never told me a word about getting letters from Bert Garr!

"I answered two of them," she said.

"Really?" He gave her a loving, hopeful look, and I rapidly surmised that that was why Nancy had decided to come on this trip with me. That was the spectacular synchronicity at work at the sidewalk café. She'd been looking for Bert, and he had found her.

"No wonder you never got them, if you move every week," she said with a smile.

"You'll have to stay here for the time being, Bert," Nick said. He didn't get any argument from Bert.

We all, except Bert, had some more coffee while we discussed the problem. Nick thought that since Conan had salvaged his honor by beating up Bert, the affair was over.

"Providing you stay away from Maria," Nancy added.

"Don't worry. You won't catch me hanging out at her gallery again. About your pictures, Nick—I don't have them. Why don't you give that Boisvert guy in Paris a buzz? Maybe he can forward the pictures you left with him. Seems a shame to lose out on the Lingini deal. I mentioned fifty thou, in Yankee dollars, and she didn't blink an eye."

"That's worth a call," Nick agreed, and left the room. The only phone in the house as far as I had seen was the red one in his studio. He came back in about ten minutes. "Boisvert's away on holidays. His wife's expecting him back in a week. I asked him to call me."

"You could splatter up half a dozen of those modern blobs in a week," Bert said. "Make a good retrospective show."

Nick considered this a moment, making me realize he was not one of those art-for-art's-sake types. "I'd have to buy the acrylics and canvas. I don't have any of them around nowadays. Besides, the pictures would look brand new. Lingini's knowledgeable. She'd know the difference."

"You could varnish them, or blow smoke on them— stick 'em in the oven for an hour. There must be some way to do a quick aging job on acrylic."

Nick laughed, and we just sat around talking, waiting to see if Bert was well enough to do the sightseeing we'd planned. Nick brought out some photographs of his first exhibit in Paris, to show us what his earlier French Frustration period was like. It was as he'd described it, angry slashes of primary color, but not splashed on in gobs. It was refined, with narrow slashes, and much crossing of lines and edges of impasto.

"It's derivative," he admitted. "Mondrian in a bad mood, and very impatient. This style has fallen out of fashion."

"Oh, I don't know," Nancy said thoughtfully. "We still saw work like that on exhibition in Paris. Remember that Frageau exhibition, Lana?"

"Frageau? I never heard of him," Nick said.

"There's a reproduction of one of his paintings right in this magazine I was looking at a minute ago. He calls it Opus 7. He entitles all his paintings by number." She riffled through the magazine and handed it to Nick, open at the proper page.

"Pretentious," Nick scoffed, but he took the magazine for a closer look. His reaction was like a double take from a silent film. His initial disinterested glance turned to one of riveted attention. His brows drew together and he made a strangled "arggh" sound. "*It's mine!* That's my *Rouge et Noir* study! That son of a bitch!"

We all gathered round to view the reproduction. It was a full-page spread—a good, glossy print. "Tempest in a teapot," Bert said. "Those exploding firecracker pictures all look alike."

"Oh, no," Nancy said firmly, "that's definitely a Frageau. I recognize the brushwork. Remember, Lana, we were wondering how he did it, and I thought he used a very full brush, with a ruler to build up that dynamic edge of impasto—unusual in acrylics. It's more common with oils." Nancy had inundated me with many of these insider's tricks during our tours of galleries and museums.

Nick continued staring at the reproduction. "To hell it's a Frageau. It's mine. And I didn't use a ruler. I used masking tape for the straight edge. Acrylic dries quickly. You can do that."

Nancy examined the picture again. "It says Frageau," she said, pointing out the signature.

"I don't care if it says Picasso! I know my own work. He's painted over my signature." Nick ran to his studio and came back with a magnifying glass. "No, he hasn't either. What he's done is cut an inch off the bottom of the canvas and ruined the balance in the process. There used to be a heavy black line close to the bottom. You notice this looks top heavy."

Nancy immediately imagined the composition was unbalanced. "This is *awful*!" she exclaimed. "What are you going to do, Nick?"

"Who's got the picture now?" He read the fine print. "From the collection of Monsieur Pierre Duplessis, Paris. He's a noted collector!"

"It mentions Georges St. Felix also has a couple," Nancy said. "The famous parfumier. Now that I think of it, Frageau is a made-up kind of a name."

"Half Fragonard, half Watteau," I offered, though of course the Frageau-Hansen painting wasn't in that old world, romantic style.

Bert was unhappy at being abandoned. "God, my gut hurts."

Nancy patted his hand, without even looking at him. "Poor Bert. Boy, I am just *full* of synchronicity," she added. "I mean going to the Frageau exhibition, and now this."

Bert listened, and decided the picture was Nick's after all. "Boisvert's pulling the old dead artist trick. The artist dies, and the price shoots through the ceiling. Supply and demand. Does it say Frageau's dead?"

"If it doesn't, it soon will," Nick seethed. "I'll kill that son of a bitch of a Boisvert. I bet he was selling my pictures when I was in Paris, and keeping my money."

"Did he have that kind of reputation?" I asked.

"He didn't have any. I couldn't get a reputable dealer to handle me."

Nancy skimmed the article and said, "Sure enough. Frageau died tragically at the age of thirty-three, leaving a small but cherished legacy. It mentions he was a heavy drug user. This does look kind of nightmarish."

I shot a worried glance at Nick. A drugee? "It's just frustration," he insisted.

Bert sat up and frowned. "Time to put on the old thinking cap. The thing to do is call Duplessis and what's his name, the perfumer. Want me to do it, Nick? I'll threaten to sic our legal department on them. Hell, they won't know we don't have any lawyers."

Nick's beautiful, sensitive face had turned to stone, in which his black eyes blazed. "Oh no," he said in a voice of silken menace, "the thing to do is find Boisvert."

"But he's on holiday. Did his wife say where?" Nancy asked.

"No, but that would be because I made the mistake of leaving my name. If he's selling my stuff under a phoney name, he must be getting very nervous. This is the latest issue of *Art World*. I haven't heard of Frageau before. Now that my alter ego is becoming known, Boisvert must be eager to fine me."

"Maybe that's who was in your kitchen yesterday!" Nancy exclaimed. "Was he a small, dark man?"

"No, he was a big, gray-haired guy, with a honker like Charles de Gaulle," Bert said. "He's in some of those pictures you were showing the girls, isn't he, Nick?"

Nancy and I had been reduced to "girls" on a couple of occasions. I meant to take them to task for it, but this didn't seem the moment. We sorted through the pictures, and Nick pointed Boisvert out to us. I had never seen him before, but I remembered hearing French at the Quattrocento yesterday afternoon. "That contessa—she was speaking French to a dark-haired, small man," I mentioned. "And she was interested in one of Nick's early works."

Nick looked interested. "He could be Boisvert's henchman."

"The Contessa wouldn't be mixed up in anything like that," Bert said. "She's top drawer."

"I'm not saying she's mixed up in it," I countered. "I'm just pointing out there was a Frenchman at the exhibition. Though now that you mention it, it *is* kind of funny that Lingini was asking for one of Nick's early works."

"Naah," Bert said dismissively. "I think I brought the subject up myself. She was talking about his tempura method, and I said he used to use acrylics. She said she'd like to get hold of one—something like that."

"That's *tempera*, Bert," Nancy said.

"Yeah, right. Imagine the Contessa not knowing that. I could hardly keep a straight face when she said it. But mainly she's interested in the gray picture with the mountains and the old house."

"Maybe we should all go back to the exhibition at the Quattrocento," I suggested, looking at Nick.

"It's some place to start," he agreed with an approving smile that warmed the cockles of my heart. "How about you, Bert? You'll stay here?"

"Alone?"

Nancy looked at us, then she looked at Bert. Compassion won. "I'll stay with you, Bert," she said.

He measured up Nancy's shoulders and, deciding she was no match for Conan, opted to go with me and Nick. "We better all stick together."

We went, together, in the Alfa-Romeo to the Quattrocento Hotel. I was wrong about the car not having any hubcaps. There must have been one on one of the back wheels, because I heard a louder than usual clanging sound behind us, and saw a chrome circle rolling down the road behind us.

CHAPTER 5

Morning isn't the busiest time for art exhibitions at home, but in Rome, where heat closes the city down for the afternoon, there was a small crowd looking around the gallery. Alberto, the Italian student manning the door, was looking dapper in a blue suit. He had a smattering of various languages, but English wasn't his best tongue, so Nick spoke to him and Bert translated for us.

Nick asked Alberto if he had seen a small, swarthy Frenchman hanging around that morning. He hadn't. Had he seen a French guy that looked like Charles de Gaulle? Not that day, but late yesterday afternoon . . . perhaps the tall gentleman with the large nose spoke French. He could not be certain—so many guests—but there was a noticeable resemblance to de Gaulle. Had he left a name, an hotel address? No, he had made only a brief visit, looking for a friend. Did the friend have a name? Very likely, but the man had not mentioned it. But really, Alberto was almost positive now that the tall man had spoken French.

Nick's eyes blazed with the thrill of the chase. "Boisvert's in town," he told us, with a menacing and infinitely delighted grin. "The game's afoot, ladies."

"He won't be easy to find in a city this size," I pointed out.

"He'll come back to the gallery eventually."

"Has to. Scene of the crime," Bert explained. "Not that

53

I mean he stole anything here . . ." Bert never could deny himself a cliché.

"Are you going to hang out here, then?" I asked. The paintings were lovely, Nick was lovelier, but neither was ravishing enough to entice me to sit in a hotel for very long, especially when Naples was waiting, prepaid.

"We'll have lunch here, and I'll check back with Alberto after. If any Frenchmen show up, he'll come and tell me in the dining room. The Quattrocento is famous for its cuisine," Nick promised.

"It's not even noon yet."

"I hate watches," Nick scowled. "What's this weird obsession with time?" It was the voice of a man who had never had a nine-to-five job, lucky devil. "We'll have a drink first. In Rome, we make a ritual of the midday meal and drink lots of wine with it."

"That would explain a great deal," I said, thinking of all the terrible drivers in Rome, and idly of Bert's problem, and Luigi's solution for that matter. Beating up poor Bert wouldn't solve anything.

We agreed to stay. The kitchen's fame, if indeed it was famous, was well deserved. The Castelli white wine slipped effortlessly down the throat. It was mellow in taste, but powerful in effect. My risotto di scampi was to die for. Fresh scampi, and they didn't cut it into slivers. There were mouth-filling, juicy chunks flavored with bay leaves, garlic, olive oil, and wine. The zabaione I had for dessert was runny, but delicious. After the feast, I didn't really care if I never got to Naples. The subject did come up over our cappuccino, however.

"You won't want to leave town at this time, Nick," I said. "Nancy and I will take a bus or train and go on to Naples."

Bert looked at me as though I were insane. "You're not leaving!"

Nancy was shifting uncomfortably, which told me she had been scheming behind my back. "That was the plan," I reminded them both.

"But don't you want to help Nick?" Nancy asked.

Nick lifted his eyebrows and looked adorably helpless.

"I suppose we could rejoin the tour at Salerno," I said hesitantly.

"I'll drive you," Nick eagerly interjected. "It'll be more comfortable than the public bus."

"A donkey cart would be more comfortable than the way you drive," I pointed out.

"I'll get my car tuned up. We haven't had time for our sightseeing. We were going to take you to the Sound and Light show at the Forum. I'm sure to get this business straightened out with Boisvert today, and we'll have tomorrow . . ."

"Boisvert may not show up for days. He may not show up at all. You don't even know for sure if he's here." While the words were leaving my mouth, Alberto came pelting into the dining room.

"Francese!" he exclaimed. A Frenchman was in the gallery, looking all around. Not the de Gaulle *francese*, but the other one.

"Let's go!" Bert said, and flicked his fingers for the bill, which he promptly handed to Nick.

"Wouldn't it be wiser to follow him, and see if he leads us to Boisvert?" Nancy suggested.

"Why don't we take a quick peek and see if it's the same man who was talking to Lingini yesterday?" I suggested. "If it is, if he's come back, I mean—well it might mean something."

"I'll go with you and see if he's the guy from the kitchen," Nancy added. "If he is, that'll clinch it."

No one objected, so while Nick paid the bill, Nancy and I went to the doorway and peeked in from behind the urns of flowers, in case he recognized us. It looked like the same man who had been with Lingini, and now that I suspected his interest in art was criminal, I thought he looked less genteel than before. His nose was slightly twisted to one side, and he had shifty eyes. It seemed suspicious that he kept a closer watch on the doorway than the pictures. "I can't be positive, but I think he's the man from the kitchen," Nancy said.

"I'm quite positive he's Lingini's friend."

I reported this back to Nick. He decided we would wait in the lobby till the man left, and follow him. Bert bought a newspaper, which we separated to allow all four of us to hide behind a section while we plotted and talked. Our conversation was carried on in whispers behind our newspaper wall.

"Have you figured out what's going down here, Nick?" Bert asked out of the side of his mouth like a gangster. "Boisvert's found out somehow where you live."

"I'm in the phone book."

"That could be how he found out. Then he sent his henchman to your place to steal the old pictures. They're worth a fortune as Frageaus. I knew I didn't have them. They were always in your studio. The guy got them, and when we came home, we caught him off guard. Nance said he came into the kitchen right after we left. That means he was already in the house. He must have been hiding in your pantry. He heard us say we were going to have a drink, and spiked something. Well, except for your wine cellar, gin and Campari are all you keep. He probably spiked them both. Then when we were all in dreamland, he took the pictures and vamoosed."

"Did Boisvert know you were coming to Italy when you left Paris, Nick?" I asked.

"Sure, I told him. I even wrote to him a couple of times. But I don't see how he hopes to get away with this. He can't expect me to sit still while my pictures are sold and published in art magazines with some other guy's name on them."

"I'll bet they sold for plenty, too," Nancy added. "I mean, Georges St. Felix—he probably paid thousands for his."

"Whoever buys the ones they stole from Nick will pay a hell of a lot more," Bert said. "Frageau's supposed to be dead, and that'll shoot the price through the ceiling. Supply and demand," he explained, and unfortunately added, "Supply-side economics. He must have some plan to keep you quiet, Nick."

While the rest of us digested this, Bert continued blandly, "Dead men tell no tales. He came here to kill you. Must be some reason he keeps hanging around the gallery. Or possibly he'll try to talk you into going along with the scam for a cut."

"He knows where I live," Nick pointed out. "He hasn't contacted me. And why should I bother painting Frageaus when my Hansens sell for more?"

"Right, looks like stiff city for you, my friend."

Nick's eyes glazed in a kind of emotional paralysis.

"Bert, for heaven's sake!" I scolded.

"Wake up and smell the cappuccino, Lana," was his bored reply. "The guy's already killed once. This Frageau dude—he's history, right? Boisvert needed a stooge to pose as the artist, so he offed some guy named Frageau."

I considered this unlikely hypothesis a moment, and looked to Nick for his opinion. "Could be," Nick said doubtfully. "Or he could have just checked out the morgue and claimed an unidentified body when he needed a dead artist."

This, while reprehensible, was at least not murder. "That's probably what he did," I decided.

Bert's paper suddenly rustled to attention. "Is he coming?" I whispered.

"No, it's Luigi," Nick said.

"Who?"

"Conan."

I peered and saw a giant striding through the lobby toward the gallery. It seemed appropriate that he had two names. He was too big for just one. He had shoulders like the Parthenon, a big barrel chest, and was so muscle-bound that he walked like a robot. His hair was taffy blond and no doubt he had cruel eyes behind those sinister black glasses.

"I'm out of here. I'm gone. Meet you back at your place, Nick," Bert whispered.

As soon as Conan-Luigi went into the gallery, Bert got up, grabbed Nancy by the hand and they disappeared down the corridor.

"He's already beat Bert up once today. Why is he still after him?" I asked.

"Did the man's face look rational to you?"

"I didn't get much of a look at his face. With a body like that . . ."

"You're susceptible to muscles?" Nick asked with an amused smile. "Now that surprises me. I thought you'd be the type that goes for brainy weaklings. I was going to buy a pair of glasses."

"You can't help noticing a giant. I don't go for the Godzilla type myself."

"What type do you go for, Lana?"

"I don't go for types. I go for individuals."

"We're all of one type or another. Macho, tortured genius . . ."

"As a general type then, rich millionaires," I said offhandedly.

"As opposed to poor millionaires. You *did* say you're an English teacher? There's a type for you."

The patter of hastening footsteps alerted us that someone was fleeing. As the floor wasn't trembling, I didn't think it was Conan. We looked over our papers and saw the Frenchman darting along, not toward the main door, but toward a side hall.

"He must be staying at this hotel. He isn't leaving," I said.

"He might be," Nick said. "He's going toward the side exit to the parking lot. He must have a car."

We waited till he was past us and then went out after him. He was talking to a uniformed hotel employee. "I bet he's asking for a taxi," I said.

"I'll slip out another door and bring the car around. You watch which way he goes—try to hear what he tells the driver."

"Right. Wait—I don't speak Italian."

"Try to remember the sounds."

The first going awry of our plan was that the man didn't call a taxi. The hotel parking service brought a little black car to the door. The man got in, naturally without telling the attendant where he was going. He just zoomed away. Nick wasn't far behind him.

"He went that way," I said, pointing to the left. "Driving a little black car."

"What kind? What make? Year?"

"Small, newish."

Nick gave me a defeated look. There were approximately fifty newish, small black cars in the river of automobiles that filled the road. But at least I knew which direction he was headed, so we could ignore the twenty-five of them going the other way. Nick took his Kamikaze pilot position at the wheel, neck craned into the windshield, white knuckles clenched on the wheel, and revved his car up to about a million miles an hour.

"You look in car windows as we pass. Tell me when you spot the Frenchman," Nick said.

What I saw as we passed was mainly a sun-streaked blur, and that only when I got up courage to open my eyes. The street we were on was extremely busy. To get into less perilous traffic, I decided one small black car turning a corner contained a Frenchman. Nick squealed around the corner, but when we finally overtook the car, it proved to hold an elderly man and woman.

"It looks like we lost him," I said, shaking my head to indicate sorrow, but I was relieved to still be alive after the death drive.

Nick pulled into a no-parking zone and stopped. "You could get a ticket here," I pointed out.

"Oh, is that what the sign says?" he asked with only minimal interest.

"You're looking right at it!"

"I'm short-sighted. In the rush, I forgot to put on my glasses. I do have a pair." He took a pair of tinted shades out of his pocket and put them on.

"You mean you couldn't even see in that traffic!"

"I can see big things, like cars. I'm not blind."

"You can't be far from it if you can't read that sign." I wiped a film of nervous perspiration from my forehead and said, "Are those prescription sunglasses?" He nodded. "Good. Let's go home—slowly."

Nick put his head back on the headrest. I had the feeling he had closed his eyes. His relaxed voice suggested it. "I'm just trying to think where Boisvert might be. You know, if he ever mentioned any friends in Rome . . ."

"Could you do this thinking in a parking zone?"

"Legal parking's very difficult here, especially in summer, but to satisfy you . . ." He pulled forward a few yards beyond the no-parking signs. He was now blocking a driveway. No one seemed to require the driveway at that moment, so I said nothing. The random thought occurred to me that Nick must be vain, or he'd wear his glasses.

When a truck came down the driveway between two stores, Nick decided to move on. "We might as well go back to my place and regroup."

I gave up trying to follow our route, all the streets seemed the same, they were so busy. At one intersection, busier than most, Nick suddenly decided to run through a light that had just turned red. Brakes squealed. Fists shook out of windows. Curses rent the air, including my personal air space in the car.

"What the hell do you think you're doing!"

"Didn't you see him? That was him, in that Jag!" Nick shouted triumphantly.

I hadn't seen him, but as the Jag weaved through traffic at a dangerous speed, I assumed Nick was right. It was also clear that we had been spotted. The car was certainly trying to avoid us. We followed the darned black Jag through the maelstrom of city traffic to the edge of town—a harrowing adventure that threatened to cost me my sanity. When the streets narrowed to alleys and the pavement to very rough cobblestone, the car turned a corner into one of the alleys.

Nick followed. It was about a block ahead of us, and we didn't know which way it had turned, but we knew it had turned because it was suddenly no longer ahead of us. At the speed blind Nick was travelling, stopping at the next intersection was impossible, but he slowed down to a crawl to see if we could spot the car. That's when the bullets started whistling. They came from the right. I didn't realize they were bullets at first. There was a sharp, loud pinging sound on Nick's door, which I thought was a kid throwing a stone. This misconception was supported by the fact that there were some kids playing around an old moss-green, graffiti-decorated fountain in the shape of a turtle that was attached to the side of one of the buildings.

"Holy Christ!" Nick exclaimed. He threw his arm around my shoulders and pulled me down on the floor, shielding me with his lean body. I was in total confusion. This seemed an excessive reaction to a kid throwing a stone. Before I uttered any of the sarcastic speeches that popped to mind, there was another sharp sound.

That one was unmistakably a bullet. It came through the side window and parted Nick's hair, before leaving by my window. If he hadn't ducked and pulled me down, one of us would have gotten a bullet through the head. We crouched on the floor and exchanged a terrified look.

"Are you all right?" he asked, and pulled off his dark glasses, which had come askew.

I did a swift mental inventory of my body. Nothing hurt except my toes, which bore a heavy load in the crouching position we were in. "I don't seem to be bleeding. Are you okay?"

"Other than being paralyzed by fear—what's that?" There was another bullet shot, this one on the fender.

"He's trying to shoot out your tires so we can't drive!"

"Christ! We've got to get out of here."

"Don't sit up!"

"Don't worry. I won't."

His solution was to drive from the floor, his eyes well below window level. Without lifting his head, Nick stepped on the gas and we drove through the intersection, fortunately without hitting any children or buildings.

Once safely beyond the intersection, he sat up and drove as fast as the traffic allowed, with me urging him on to go faster. I was certainly hysterical. The maniacal laughter issuing from my gullet sounded like the wail of a banshee.

Nick was white as a ghost, and rigid, and angry. The Jag didn't follow us.

"Where are we?" he asked—one of the season's most useless questions.

"Roma, the last I heard."

After straggling through alleys for a quarter of an hour, we hit a street Nick recognized and from there we went directly to his house. As the panic subsided, we tried to make sense of it.

"Bert was right. The plan *is* for Boisvert to kill me," Nick said in a high, disbelieving voice. "My God—*kill me*. That's why they've been skulking around the exhibition."

"Cheerful thought, but that wasn't Boisvert."

"It was his henchman. Had to be. I don't have any enemies. Sorry, Lana. I shouldn't have tried to keep you here. I had no idea Boisvert played this rough. Oh, I knew he was no saint, but I never imagined he'd turned into a full-fledged criminal. The lure of gold . . . It might be the safest thing for you and Nancy to take a bus to Naples. I'm not sure this car is safe."

We looked at the twin bullet holes, one in either window. The wind made a light whistling sound as it entered. "Even without hitmen shooting at it, this car is a lethal weapon. I guess you'll be going to the police, huh?" I asked.

"I really should," he said doubtfully. "Did you happen to get that license number?"

To my shame, I couldn't even tell you its color. "No."

"Neither did I. But the car was a Jag—wasn't it?"

"How would I know?"

"It looked like a Jag—sort of."

"We could identify the man. At least I could."

"But then you'd have to stay in Rome," he said with a slyly flirtatious smile. His hand reached across the seat and squeezed mine. "Yes, I really must report this attack."

CHAPTER 6

But first he wanted to talk it over with Bert and Nancy. We went into the villa on legs that wobbled like Jell-O.

Bert was nursing a Coke, and Nancy was looking at some of Nick's art books. "We made it home in one piece," Bert assured us.

"We nearly didn't," Nick told him, and related the story.

Bert listened, as impassive as a cigar store Indian. You'd think his best friend was shot at every day of the week. Only his eyes betrayed any excitement, and told me this act was to make him look debonair in front of Nancy. Nancy, of course, was all gasps and sympathy.

"I warned you Boisvert'd be after you," Bert said, shaking his head. "You'll have to lay low awhile, Nick."

"He's going to the police," I said firmly.

"Of course, but they're not going to get ahold of Boisvert in one day," Bert pointed out. "Boisvert knows where Nick lives. You're a sitting duck, my man. Might not be a bad idea for you to go to a hotel."

"But which hotel? Where is Boisvert staying?" Nick asked, though chasing Boisvert wasn't what Bert meant. Nick closed his eyes, as though waiting for a vision. "Where they always turn up is at my exhibition."

"Then that's where you should have the police go," I suggested, as no one seemed to be talking about police.

"I doubt if they'll go back there now, after shooting at

you," Nancy said. "They'll know the cops'll be waiting for them."

Nick nodded. "That's the trouble once you call in police. They're all over, scaring people away. I think Bert and I can handle this."

I gave him a look suggesting that they couldn't handle an angry kitten.

"Wish I could help you," Bert said. "But with Luigi lurking in the grass to attack me . . ."

"Why would he have gone looking for you this afternoon, after he beat you up this morning?" Nancy asked.

"Beating guys up is his hobby. The man's an animal," Bert said with an involuntary shudder that revealed his real fear.

Nick had gone back to his interrupted vision while we talked. He now opened his eyes and spoke. "What we have to do is smoke Boisvert out."

A nervous spasm shook my insides. "How?" I asked warily.

"Con brio."

"With cheese?" Nancy asked, looking quite lost.

"And onions."

"You've lost me," I admitted.

"I should be so lucky," Nick said, but his lambent smile removed the sting. "Lingini was talking to that Frenchman who shot at us."

"Maybe if you talked to her, she'd know where he's staying," I said. "But you don't want to make it too obvious, in case she's working with them. She *did* ask Bert for one of your old paintings."

"Want me to give her a call?" Bert asked.

"It might be worth a shot," Nick replied.

"Hey, I've got a better idea!" Bert exclaimed. "Why don't I drop in on her unexpectedly? Maybe she'll have company—know what I mean? The Frenchie. Maybe even Boisvert. I'd recognize him, but he has no way of knowing that."

Nancy wasn't happy with this idea. "You said Lingini isn't mixed up in it, Bert."

"She might know something," Bert said. "It's worth a shot. Only take thirty minutes. And there's no way Luigi'll be waiting for me at a contessa's place. I wouldn't mind getting a look at her digs."

"Her butler won't even let you in the door," Nancy sniffed.

"Watch and learn," Bert said. "I'll phone first for an appointment."

We didn't watch, or even listen, since the only phone was in the studio. He was back in minutes. "She was falling all over me," he said, with a "so there" look at Nancy. "Invited me to Villa Lingini—it's up in the Pincian Hill somewhere. Can I borrow your wheels, Nick? The scooter?"

"Take the car if you like."

"Not a good idea with Boisvert's henchman out gunning for you. Besides, if Luigi spots me, it's easier to get away on a scooter. You can shoehorn that little sucker through traffic like anything."

"Why don't you get your own car, Bert? It's still at your apartment," Nancy suggested.

"It's broken down. The rad's shot, I think. I'll have to have it fixed. The student I'm renting my apartment to wants the parking space."

I already knew Bert wasn't doing well financially from the rat's nest he had lived in, but if he couldn't even afford to get his car repaired, he must really be suffering.

"What are you going to say to Lingini?" I asked. With Bert, it's a good idea to check these things.

"I'll tell her Nick has a few of his old expressionist paintings in storage. Hasn't managed to unearth them yet, but is she still interested? Then I'll drop a hint that a French gent has been asking after them as well. See if she flinches. Maybe she'll crop out with a name."

If the Contessa was involved, it wasn't likely she'd blurt out any names and addresses, but if she thought her henchmen were trying to double-cross her and get the paintings themselves—well, it was worth a try.

"Try the name Boisvert on her," Nick suggested with an expression that would have done Machiavelli justice.

"And if she bites?"

"Just note her reaction."

"You guys are out of it," Nancy said grandly. "What you do is lurk around outside when you leave. Then if she runs out to her car, you follow her. Listening at keyholes to hear if she phones somebody is good, too, but that'd be hard at a villa, with servants and everything."

Bert beamed proudly. "Has this girl got brains, or what?"

"I read Nancy Drew when I was a kid," Nancy explained. "Hey! More synchronicity—we have the same name."

There seemed no sane comment to make on this.

Bert put on the black driving helmet and left, looking like Darth Vadar in mufti. Over his shoulder he called, "You gals'll still be here when I get back?"

We agreed to wait another half hour. Leaving before the mystery was solved seemed less exigent now that we were safely back in Nick's villa.

"We'll do that sightseeing this afternoon," Nick said.

Sightseeing in a broken-down car that was a target for bullets with a semi-blind driver besides, had very limited appeal.

"We're missing the Naples tour," I said, but uncertainly.

"We can case Naples on our way through to Salerno," Nancy suggested. She hadn't used words like "case" before we met up with Bert.

"Yes. Are you going to call the police now, Nick?"

"What do you say we have some cappuccino on the terrace while we wait for Bert to come back?" he answered. "Maybe we'll know by then whether the Contessa is involved." And if she was, he'd say there was no point trying to get the police to help a bunch of Americans catch one of their own contessas. "I'll make it. You two go on out and catch some sun."

Nancy and I went out. One side of the terrace got the afternoon sun, but we decided to sit on the shady side, where a view of Rome spread out below us. The terra-cotta rooftops gleamed in the heat. Striations rippled up from them, turning the air wavy. Traffic had slowed noticeably. It was siesta time in Rome.

Nancy said, "What we were talking about in there, Lana—about Conan still looking for Bert when he'd already beat him up—it is kind of strange, isn't it?"

"It's his hobby."

"That's ridiculous. And there's no denying Bert has a few twists in him. Nick thought Bert must have taken those expressionist paintings. Bert runs tame here. He could have taken them."

"That has nothing to do with Conan beating him. That business is over a woman—Maria, Conan's friend."

"Yes," she said doubtfully, "but maybe Conan's involved somehow, too. I was thinking maybe Boisvert got in touch with Bert, and asked him for the expressionist paintings. Bert wouldn't necessarily say no to a little illegal business on the side. He thought those early paintings were practically worthless. He's obviously having trouble making ends meet. That apartment! And his car doesn't work."

The image of Bert's hovel of an apartment wafted through my mind. I remembered the notice over his sink saying that anyone can become a millionaire. "That still doesn't tie Conan and Boisvert together. Why are you suddenly putting Bert under a microscope? Not that he doesn't belong there, but I thought you liked him. Did he say something while we were gone?"

"Not exactly. What he said was he hoped Nick didn't get the idea he'd double-crossed him. He said he stood to make a lot more as Nick's agent than he'd ever get selling a few of his older paintings. Why did he say that? It was almost as if he was denying something nobody had accused him of. It just made me wonder. Bert's very naive, in a way. He called our attention to his Gucci watch being a knockoff before anyone even noticed it. I mean, he cuts the ground out from under his own feet. If he was working with Boisvert, he could get a lot more than fifteen percent. Probably fifty."

Her concern made me wonder, too. It was exactly the sort of chiseling, sneaky larceny Bert was capable of. When

Nick brought out the cappuccino, I asked idly, "Does Boisvert know Bert's your agent now? Is it the proper thing to notify your old agent when you change?"

"I dropped him a line. Bert said I should notify him officially. I did have a written contract with the guy, but either of us could end it at any time. I sent Boisvert a registered letter. Why are you asking?"

"I just wondered."

Nick took his cup and leaned back in a lounge chair, sipping his coffee while he thought. "You think Bert's already sold the paintings that disappeared from my studio?"

"Oh no!" we exclaimed in unison.

Nick examined us, one by one, with a knowing eye. "I don't think so either. If Bert had sold my old stuff, Boisvert wouldn't have sent his man to check out my studio. I figure Boisvert's man got the paintings all right. Bert didn't know they were worth anything till yesterday, when the Contessa tipped him off. And from that point on, he didn't have a chance at them. We were together. I trust Bert implicitly. We're friends, but I'm just mentioning this as you apparently have some doubts."

We made unconvincing sounds of objection, and Nick continued. "What concerns me more is that I'm expendable. Better off dead, as far as Boisvert is concerned. Quite apart from the money involved, Boisvert's reputation would be shot if this ever came out, and art is his life."

Nancy and I exchanged a relieved look. Of course. If Bert had sold Boisvert all of Nick's early works, they wouldn't have had to break in. Unless they thought Bert was holding some back . . . Damn, there was no end to it.

Bert had seemed very anxious to see Lingini. He was the one who'd suggested going to see her. I'd first mentioned her name, but he'd offered to phone—then go in person. Maybe because he was afraid we'd go and listen to his phone conversation? Yesterday he said she definitely wasn't involved. When Bert got back, I meant to have a go at him. His face used to turn bright red when he lied. It's hard to control that kind of involuntary reaction. I thought I'd know if he was lying.

During the next half hour we gave Nancy a blow-by-blow description of our morning, and took her to see the bullet holes in the car. "My God, how come you weren't killed, Nick? They're right where your head was." There was one through my side window, too, but maybe she didn't see it.

"Free air-conditioning. A good thing it wasn't the windshield or I'd have to get it fixed," was Nick's comment.

We had another cappuccino, and dawdled over it till four. Bert had been gone over an hour. Half an hour was what he thought it would take. Edginess turned to apprehension as we sat, avoiding each other's eyes. In my mind Bert, possible traitor, had become Bert, possible victim—again.

"Maybe one of us should just give Lingini a call and see if Bert got there all right," I suggested idly, not wanting to upset Nancy.

She was already upset. "Conan might have waylaid him."

"We don't speak Italian, Nick," I pointed out.

"The Contessa's a linguist. She speaks English, as well as German and French, and of course Italian."

"Why don't you want to phone her?"

"It might be better if you call—tell her you're a friend of Bert's."

"You help me find her number in the phone book," I said.

Nancy stayed on the terrace when Nick followed me into the house. "Why don't you really want to speak to her?" I asked.

"Because if what you and Nancy think is right, that Bert's double-crossing me, I'm not supposed to know anything about it. Maybe I'm not even supposed to know he's seeing her today. Let's just keep it that way for the time being."

After I thought about it for a minute, I said, "It sounds as if you're trying to protect Bert, even if he's double-crossing you."

"I don't think he is. Bert's always been a loyal friend to me. Good friends are hard to find. It has nothing to do with having things in common really. A friend is someone whose company you enjoy. From the minute I pulled Bert out of the drink and he said, 'Thanks, old buddy,' I felt sympatico with him. That night we got drunk together, and he told me all about himself. I told him my life story, too. We felt very sorry for ourselves, and each other."

"He's always been easy to talk to."

"And confide in. I never feel Bert's looking down his nose at me. In fact, he looks up a little more than I'm comfortable with. Maybe I enjoy that, too. He's always here to help me, and I help him. After you've helped someone, there's a kind of bonding. I guess Bert has become the brother I never had. He means that much to me, anyway."

"And you trust him." I nodded.

"If he did anything slightly illegal, he only intended to chisel a few bucks from paintings that he thought weren't worth much. I don't believe he even did that. Bert confesses things—you know? I don't want to get the poor guy shot. And if Lingini and Boisvert are working together, and they get the idea Bert's there fishing for information on my behalf—well . . . those were real bullets that were whistling through my car a few hours ago."

I gulped. "Gosh!"

He grinned. "You English teachers are so articulate."

He dialed the phone, handed me the receiver, and stuck his head beside mine to overhear the conversation. As soon as I spoke English, the man who answered put me right through to Lingini. I heard the tinkling of her gold bracelets before she spoke. She spoke perfect English, with an English accent.

I identified myself as an American friend of Bert Garr. "Oh, are you one of the ladies who was with him at the gallery yesterday?" she asked.

"Yes, he was supposed to meet me half an hour ago at my hotel." I decided to give the impression that's where I was calling from. "He said he was going to see you—something about a painting. Since he's so late, I just wondered if he was still there."

"No, he left half an hour ago," she said.

Nick covered the mouthpiece and whispered in my ear. "Ask her if she liked the painting."

"Did you like the painting?" I asked, frowning at Nick. This was his way of confirming that Bert wasn't selling the paintings behind his back.

"Painting? Oh he didn't have it with him. He thinks he can get me one. I look forward to seeing it. Will you be with Mr. Garr this evening?"

I was thrown into confusion by this question, but said, "Perhaps. My tour is leaving soon for Naples."

A silver tinkle of laughter came along the wire, as clearly as if the Contessa sat right beside me. "How stupid of me! Of course he hasn't told you yet. He promised to bring Mr. Hansen to my little gala this evening. A few friends are coming around—drinks, perhaps dancing on the terrace if the weather continues fine. I told him to bring his American friends. I hope you can fit it into your schedule."

"Thank you. We'd love to come."

We rang off, very civilly. "He left half an hour ago, Nick. Where can he be?"

I hadn't seen Nancy hovering at the door, but she heard me and wailed, "Conan's got him again!"

"We'd better go rescue him," Nick said, and we all ran to the car.

CHAPTER 7

Our timing couldn't have been worse. Roman traffic was back in full swing after its daily siesta. The city crawled by, a pastiche of old ochre buildings, crumbling stone fountains, policemen, pedestrians, cars, noise and motorbikes that shot out of nowhere in a desperate attempt to kill their drivers. I was surprised to learn a contessa would live in what is more or less a commercial district of shops and offices. The view, of course, was fantastic: the Piazza di Spagna spread below the famous Spanish Steps, the meeting place for tourists and half of Rome, judging from the number of bodies swarming there.

"All these used to be noblemen's townhouses," Nick explained. "That's the Contessa's there." He pointed her house out as we glided by.

Nancy and I rubbernecked to see how a contessa lived. It was a charming old russet-colored house, heavily vined and shuttered. There was a pretty stone railing with big flower-pots on top, but other than that, it could have been slipped into one of our fancier Connecticut suburbs without looking too out of place. I had been picturing old stone and columns.

"No turrets? No ramparts? No nothing?" Nancy asked, disappointed.

"The aristocracy keep a low profile in the city," Nick explained. "Their country estates are probably larger. Even this house will be fancier inside. All this land was part of

72

the Roman General Lucullus's estate in the first century B.C."

Such tidbits of ancient lore were dropped nonchalantly by the tour guides, too. It was difficult to grasp, to integrate so vast a stretch of time and history into so small an area. Caesars and Luculluses belonged in fading textbooks.

While I dreamed of history, Nancy's mind was more practically employed. "Let's park and walk past, see if we can spot Bert's motorcycle," she suggested. "The Contessa might have been lying and have him locked up."

I wanted a closer look myself and pretended to agree to this gothic hypothesis. Nick parked the car by the side of the road. I didn't see any *Vietato Il Parcheggio* signs, but I didn't see any parked cars either. We got out and crossed the street where other tourist gawkers were sightseeing, to lend us anonymity. There was a fair bit of green space around the villa, with fences concealed by vines. There were no motorbikes. Nancy ventured onto the grass and a roar of barking was set off behind the fence. What looked at a quick glance like a pack of leaping pit bull terriers' gnashing teeth appeared above the vines. I never saw Nancy move so fast before in my life. Her bosoms were bouncing like jelly.

"Why would she keep a pack of wild dogs if she isn't some kind of crook!" she huffed.

"Maybe she's a dog lover," Nick replied.

Pit bull terriers are especially noted for their tenacity. They kept up such a bellow that we decided it might be a good idea to disappear. We strolled casually back to the car at about sixty miles an hour and scooted away.

"Bert's probably back at Nick's place by now," I said, to try to cheer Nancy. She sat in the backseat, chewing her thumb and worrying. "Why don't you phone your place, Nick?"

He parked illegally, half of the car resting on the sidewalk by a phone box, and phoned. "Nope," he said, coming back to the car. "My cleaning woman's there. He hasn't showed up. We'll try his apartment."

Bert wasn't in his apartment, he wasn't in the pensione he had rented, and he wasn't at the gallery. The big question in my mind was: Was he with Boisvert, arranging some new stunt, or had Conan got him?

"I'm going to call the police," Nancy announced.

"Maybe he's home by now. We'll call them from my place if he isn't," Nick said, and drove home.

The motorbike was chained to the post in the driveway when we got there. Our relief was liberally mixed with exasperation when we went in and found Bert lolling at his ease on the sofa, sipping a cool beer. He looked up and said, "Where the devil have you guys been? I've been waiting for ages. You might have left a note at least. I bought us some beer, since the gin and Campari are probably doctored. I emptied the bottles down the sink."

It occurred to me that we could have had the dregs analyzed, but since Nick obviously had no intention of going to the police, there didn't seem much point. After the three of us had finished reviling Bert, he spread out his hands to demand silence. "Thanks for worrying about me, folks. You are very special people, all of you. Really unique. I appreciate it, but I escaped him this time."

"Conan?" Nancy asked, eyes sparkling.

"He chased me from one end of Rome to the other, but I kept ahead of him. Finally lost him in the crowds at the Colosseum. I know it inside-out from my tour days. I popped into the ladies' can, paid a guide to move the bike a block away, and got away without a scratch. Except on my shins when I climbed over the window of the john."

"What happened at Lingini's place?" Nick asked after Bert had repeated his story a few times, and pulled up his trouser leg to show Nancy the scratch. His leg was red, which sort of convinced me he was telling the truth.

"Wow! What a shack! The place looks like a quarry. Marble from one end to the other. Even the doorways are marble. Anyway, she's mighty interested in getting hold of an early Hansen. I told her we only had two, and some French guy was hot after them. 'Fellow named Boisvert,' I told her, peering from the corner of my eye. Nothing. Zilch. Zippo. She didn't bat an eyelash. 'I'll pay you more' is all she said. Didn't even ask what Boisvert was offering. That being the case . . ." he said, with a meaningful wiggle of his eyebrows.

"I'll have to get some acrylics and canvas," Nick replied.

"I'm way ahead of you. Where do you think Luigi found me? I stopped at the art shop and got all that stuff. Put it on your tab."

I noticed that Nick was planning to forge a new "old" painting, but as all his business acquaintances were crooks of one sort or another, I didn't blame him. "I thought Luigi was supposed to work at some academy or something," I said. "How come he's free to follow you all over town, Bert?"

"He has a desk and a title. It doesn't involve much work. It's known as nepotism, Lana. His uncle runs the place— state owned. Maria tells me he comes from a very influential family."

Nancy looked alert. "When did you see Maria?"

"I'm talking ancient history here," he assured her. "I haven't seen her for a couple of weeks. The family dinner she invited me to was enough to cool my passion, even without Luigi. She has five sisters, four brothers, about six dozen aunts and uncles and cousins. Oh, and four grandparents. They all get together on birthdays. There must have been eighty-nine Italians around the table, spooning pasta and gargling wine and shouting. It was like a mob scene at Cinecittà."

We all had a bottle of beer and sat around, discussing what we now called "the case." Nick felt he should be looking for Boisvert. I felt he should call the police. Nancy thought Bert should report Conan. No one mentioned Naples or Salerno. What really occupied both my and Nancy's minds was the thrilling knowledge that we were going to a party at a contessa's villa that night. Maybe Marcello Mastroianni would be there. This extremely vague possibility required a shampoo and a hairdo. It required a fresh shave of the legs and repairing of nail polish. Men had no idea how many parts of a woman's body had to be washed, shaved, polished, buffed, crimped, curled, and otherwise disguised before they could creditably appear in public.

"I'm going to shower now," Nancy said. "When and where are we eating?"

"I asked my cleaning lady to make dinner and leave it," Nick said. "It's not her day to clean, but she does some cooking for me when I have company. I thought you might like to try some real Italian cuisine."

"The ladies will be busy for hours, making themselves presentable," Bert said. "This is your chance to do the Frageau, Nick."

Nick flexed his long, artistic fingers. "I'm kind of looking forward to it. I wonder if I still know how to use acrylics."

"What are *you* going to do, Bert?" Nancy asked. "Maybe you should use this time to tend to some of your other artists."

"What other artists? I'm Nick's exclusive agent."

And obviously Nick was his exclusive artist, despite his boast of managing "a stable of artists", when he first met us. I wasn't surprised that the stable held only one horse, but Nancy looked disappointed.

"Is that all you do?" she asked.

"Of course not! I'm a freelance businessman. This brain for hire."

"What else do you do?" she persisted.

Nick and I looked away in embarrassment.

"I fill in when World Travel needs an extra guide. The tips are fantastic. I take the customers to certain shops that give me a cut. Old Bert has plenty of irons in the fire, don't you worry."

"Oh."

Nancy and I began our preparations for the party. By the time she was in full rig, our room looked as if a cyclone had torn through it, and Nancy looked as if she had stepped right off a movie screen. The blond hair tumbled around her shoulders. The pound or so of mascara on her lashes made them droopy, but in the low-slung, white floating dress, it wasn't likely any man would be looking at her eyelashes. I wore the one evening outfit I'd brought with me, viz a pale blue calf-length dress with a full skirt and braided straps. Low-key elegance was the best that could be said for it, if a viewer was feeling generous. I realized that elegance ran a poor second to sexy. Nancy used her blow dryer to entice my hair into waves. I even used mascara, which was a waste of time as I knew I'd resort to my glasses before the evening was over. I wanted to be able to see the Contessa's marble villa. My evening sandals rubbed on my healing blister, which made it necessary for me to wear two Band-Aids, and pantyhose to hold them in place.

Nick was still busy in the studio when we finished, but Bert was dressed in a white dinner jacket, which surprised me, and a red cumberbund, which didn't. "I dashed home and packed a suitcase while you ladies were dressing, since I'll be staying with Nick awhile," he explained.

He looked quite . . . presentable. He was drinking from a wineglass, leaning against a wall that gave him a view of himself in the mirror across the room. I knew he was thinking how debonair he looked, as if he'd already made his million. He gave us a practiced once-over and nodded in satisfaction.

"Very classy, Bert," I said.

He beamed his gratitude. "What, this? You really need formal duds in Europe. Especially since I'm managing Nick. I got this for his first show. And you are both looking très chic, ladies," he added. In this debonair mood, we "girls" had become "ladies." "Can I get you a glass of vino?"

We had the vino while Nick showered and dressed. He wore a navy blazer of slender cut and impeccable tailoring and looked fantastic. When he took it off to go and heat up dinner, I noticed the label said Armani.

I went to the kitchen to help him with dinner. "Are we over-dressed for this party?" I asked.

"Nowadays anything goes. There'll be everything from T-shirts to black-tie. Some of the guests will be at formal do's before they drop in. You look fine, Lana. In fact," he added with a replica of Bert's head-to-toe examination, "you look marvelous. Blue suits you. I'd like to paint you in blue."

I felt a warm blush course up my neck. "I'm flattered, but it'll have to be a quick sketch. I can't stay much longer."

"America's only a plane ride away. My father's still in America. I visit him."

My vitals began simmering as he looked at me with his liquid black eyes. "Or perhaps nude, with the blue sky behind you. In that gown, you look like a Botticelli grace. You wouldn't mind posing nude?"

While I stood with my jaw hanging, he opened the microwave and slid a big covered dish in. "In America, this would be called lamb stew," he said. "Here we call it *agnello al verdetto*. There should be a salad ready in the fridge."

I got out the salad, mostly romaine, with olives and pimento. His woman had set the dining room table before she left, and I put the wooden bowl in the middle of the rose-colored linen cloth. Everything looked beautiful—the fine china wasn't what we had used for our indoor picnic. Minton, it said on the bottom of the plate. The etched wineglass let off the tinkle of crystal when I pinged one with my finger. The cutlery was baroque-looking old sterling, and felt heavy in my hand. But all this was done on a superficial level. Inside my skull, it wasn't china and crystal and silver I was thinking about. It was me, starkers under a blue sky, posing for Nick, trying to cover all my vitals with only two hands. I didn't have long hair like Botticelli's Venus.

It was stupid to be squeamish about it. If the painting were to be done in Italy, I thought I might hack it. But in Troy, New York? I didn't hear Nick glide into the room. I didn't know he was there, behind me, till I felt his arms go around my waist, pulling me against his chest. His lips nuzzled my ear, sending gushers of lava into my chest.

"You didn't give me your answer," he murmured.

"No, I didn't, did I?" I looked at my hands, and saw I was holding one of the forks, lifted to read if it was sterling.

"It's genuine," he assured me, with a forgiving smile. "So's the china."

"I know. I've already looked." This needed some explanation. "I've always loved this kind of stuff. I look at it in antique shops and covet it. Dishes so beautiful you'd cry if you broke one."

"You don't want dishes, Lana. You want a baby you can eat off of. A great aunt left all this stuff to me when she died. It's half the reason I bought the house. They needed a home. Possessions are a great nuisance. I half wish I didn't have them."

"That sounds Freudian." He frowned. "You're the one who compared them to children. You don't want responsibilities."

"Haven't you heard, Freud is dead?"

"I thought that was God."

"Freud has outlived his usefulness, too. Someone is killing all my old friends. If I hear of Charlie Brown going down the tubes, I'll quit the human race."

"Or maybe be forced to grow up."

"Same thing, isn't it?" In the same matter-of-fact way, he continued, "It doesn't have to be nude. It was just an idea. Actually textiles can be very sensuous, too." His hands began feeling my hips, not for the sensuous quality of polyester I think.

I took a deep breath and said, "Do you think—a red wine with the casserole?"

"It's already breathing on the side table."

It was the heavy breathing in my ear that I was more aware of. Nibbling kisses invaded my neck, and his silky hair tickled my jaw. "I had planned to visit Dad for Christmas," he said softly, in that cashmere voice. "But autumn is beautiful in Massachusetts. Is it beautiful in Troy, too?"

"It's a busy time for me. School starts in September. At Christmas I have a week off." My voice was ragged.

"Good—that's long enough for you to visit me here."

A transatlantic affair had an undeniable charm to a small-town woman, but the logistics—mainly the expense—were difficult, to say the least. Already my devious mind was figuring that there wouldn't be any hotel bills to pay, just the plane fare.

Bert appeared in the doorway. "Is it nearly chow time?" he asked.

I jumped guiltily. Nick kept his arm around my waist, but lifted his head. "In a minute. You might as well sit down." Then he gazed lovingly at me, as if I were a well-seasoned dish of pasta. "We'll talk about it later," he said.

I had planned to help him serve, but was reluctant to chase him back into the kitchen. He might think I was following him. Bert sat down (without calling Nancy) and gave me a knowing look.

"I see you and Nick are beginning to hit it off. He must have pulled the old 'he'd love to paint you' stunt. What a guy. I wish I were an artist. That one gets them every time. Just a word to the wise—don't give in too easily, or he'll want to paint you au naturel."

I gave him a bored look while seething inside. I had to be rude to somebody, and poor Bert got it between the eyes. "Would your mind be able to breathe if you ever let it out of the gutter, or would the atmosphere be too rarefied for it?"

Bert laughed. "Yup, he did it."

"Aren't you going to call Nancy, or did you plan to let her starve?"

"Somebody's in a bitchy mood—and we know why."

He called Nancy, and I sat planning my revenge on Nick. The initial move was to withhold my compliments on the casserole, which was divine. Little puddles of olive oil floated on top of the sauce. Green herbs, dark from the oven, floated in the wine sauce. The smell of garlic, etc., caused my stiff mouth to water. The bread was a puff of white cloud, held in by brown crust. I nibbled silently.

"Don't you like it, Lana?" Nick asked, all eager concern.

"It's fine. Really."

Nick poured wine. I found it fine, too—really. Nancy made up in exuberance for my lack of praise. Everything was "just fabulous." By some strange synchronicity, she had just been thinking of lamb.

"I'm so glad we stayed, aren't you, Lana? I wouldn't have missed this for anything. The whole adventure, I mean, not just this fantastic meal. And tonight we're going to a party at a contessa's villa. It's like *Lifestyles of the Rich and Famous*. Boy, nothing like this ever happens in Troy."

"That's true," I agreed blandly. "Things are livelier here. I've never been shot at in Troy, not once." Nor had I ever been propositioned. I blame it on my profession.

Bert regaled us with a story of some disgruntled tourist who had threatened to kill him with a meat cleaver in Venice because the man's wife wouldn't leave Bert alone. I translated this to mean Bert had been putting the make on the man's wife.

"Where the guy got hold of a meat cleaver in Venice I don't know. Go figure. It was brand new, he bought it especially to split my head open. The dope attacked me right on the edge of the Grand Canal. One shove and he was in the sewer, up to his eyeballs in—" Nancy halted him with a gimlet look. "Still holding on to his cleaver. Most people in Venice used to buy glass. They specialize in it there. I knew a guy that'd sell me glass bead necklaces for two bits. The tourists paid a couple of bucks for them, and thought they were getting a bargain. One lady told me she paid fifteen bucks for an identical necklace in the States. I could've got it for her for two bits and made fourteen dollars and seventy-five cents profit."

Nancy helped remove the plates and Nick brought in dessert. "I had zabaione made, especially for you," he told me, setting a dish in front of me.

"You shouldn't have, Nick," I said, smiling glacially. "It separates if you leave it standing." It had split into layers, which the crystal dishes made obvious.

"Would you like some fruit instead?" he asked, becoming a little stiff about the lips himself. "Figs, nectarines— lemons?"

"I'm not really very hungry, thank you."

"An espresso? You wouldn't want to fall asleep at the Contessa's party."

"Oh, espresso! Include me out," Bert said. "That grog keeps me awake for a week."

"Espresso will be fine," I said, as I wanted to disagree with Bert. Unfortunately I hate espresso.

We finished the meal with bitter espresso, made potable in my case with plenty of cream and sugar. Nick said I was ruining it, so I added more cream. Bert had another glass of wine, then we went to make our final preparations for the party. My blisters were killing me.

CHAPTER 8

The bacchanal at the Contessa's villa was in full swing by the time we got there, and we weren't very late. I don't know whether to describe the sumptuous villa first, or the guests. The entrance hallway had a black and white marble floor, not in simple squares, but mostly white with black squares set in a pattern. A dark wood staircase with red carpeting snaked its way up on the right. As Bert said, even the doorways were marble. There were some expensive antique commodes in the hall, loaded with old Chinese vases, probably authentic Ming or something. Oh, and there was a Picasso cubist painting, blue and red and black, over one of the tables. It looked genuine. Maybe that's why she kept the pit bull terriers.

A quick peek into the room on the left showed Persian rugs and walls of cabinets, all lined with blue and white pottery. "Japanese Imari," Nancy whispered in my ear. "Gooooorgeous." There was also a gorgeous Van Gogh on the wall, of sunflowers but not the famous one that sold for millions awhile ago. Still, the dogs became more reasonable at every glance.

The ballroom was another wonder, full of chandeliers, and hung with wheat-colored damask, both walls and drapes. I didn't see any famous paintings in that room. It was probably too public. The Contessa, radiant in a shimmering wisp of silver, came swanning regally into the room. The golden bangles had been replaced by a sapphire bracelet with matching necklace. I assumed the stumpy, gray-haired little gentleman with her was the Conte. As soon as she spotted us, she came forward to make us welcome. With the nose of an aristocrat, she went straight for Nick, the only one of us with any claim to distinction in appearance. I felt like a frump, and Nancy and Bert looked as if they belonged at a Rotary banquet in Troy.

"Signor Hansen," she smiled, latching her arm through his. A volley of Italian flowed from her lips. Whatever she said set him grinning like a schoolboy. Eventually she nodded at Bert, and Nick introduced Nancy and me. The Contessa introduced her conte, who smiled graciously, and left. Then she disappeared with my escort and I trailed around the room with Bert and Nancy, ogling the guests. Nick had misled me by saying there'd be T-shirts present. A blazer was the most informal attire seen. What there were a lot of were black ties and ribbons and medals. The women mostly wore long gowns, but some had on fancy short dresses. All of them seemed to be heavily decked in glittering jewelry. They looked fussier than American women, with more elaborate hairdos and stronger perfume. Their voices were very loud.

Soon a midget with black hair and a moustache approached and had the lack of discrimination to ask me to dance. He was about up to my chin, but since he had a blue ribbon over his black jacket, I thought he must be important. Besides, Nick stuck like glue to Lingini, so I danced with the Italian munchkin. He let fly some Italian.

"Sorry, I don't speak Italian," I said. He laughed in delight, and his left hand descended to my hip.

"Now, now. None of that," I scolded merrily, yanking his hand up.

He gargled some more words and the fingers gave me a good pinch. I yelped like a stuck pig. He laughed, and danced and tried to ease me out the doorway. "You go. There are some nice doggies out there that would like to play with you," I said, and escaped back to Bert.

"I think I was dancing with a count, or minister or something," I said, pointing out my opponent.

Bert looked and shook his head. "That guy's a clerk in one of the shadier galleries," he told me.

"The creep! What was he doing with a ribbon across his chest?"

"It's got something to do with the church. Like Knights of Columbus back home. Maybe he's a Grand Knight."

"He was gift wrapped, especially for you," Nancy said and smiled.

When I was approached by another gentleman, innocent of black jacket and ribbon, I agreed to dance, but meant to keep him in line.

"I don't mambo Italiano," I warned him.

He smiled and held me a little closer, murmuring passionate phrases in my ear. When the hand began slipping hipwards, I got a half nelson on it and said through gritted teeth, "If I feel you reaching for my buns again, chum, you're going to wish you'd worn your football equipment."

He looked surprised. He understood the tone, if not the words. E'er long, the moving hand moved again and began an insidious stroking, followed by a loving pinch. I reached down and gave him a good pinch on the buttocks—which incidentally were as hard as a rock,

"Let's see how you like it, Mario," I said, and strode to the side of the room.

Bert came rushing at me. I was sure he was going to tell me I'd been dancing with a Mafioso. "Wow, that was the Foreign Minister, Lana. What'd he say?"

I was beyond caring. "How would I know? He doesn't speak English."

"Are you kidding? The guy was visiting Margaret Thatcher last week. He speaks perfect English."

"In that case, he was probably telling me he was going to have me deported. How come clerks wear ribbons on their chests, and ministers wear baggy jackets and unpressed trousers?"

"You don't have to dress up when you're rich," Bert explained, in the most perceptive comment I ever heard from him.

After we had had our fill of admiring the Contessa's

material possessions, we decided it was time to start looking for Frenchmen. A few tours of the floor told us French was not being spoken at the Villa Lingini that evening. Italian and English were the languages, mostly Italian. An Italian gentleman asked Nancy to dance, and as she thought she had seen him in a foreign film two years ago, she accepted. I was left with Bert, and was grateful for his company.

"Let's take a look at some of the house," I suggested.

We went into the hallway, but when we got a few yards along a servant appeared and asked if we required something. Bert knew enough Italian that he got the message— we were not expected to do any looking around. "You'd think we planned to steal the cutlery," he grouched.

There were enough priceless bibelots of pocket size around that the servant seemed a reasonable precaution to me. Just as we were returning to the ballroom, a door in the depths of the corridor opened and the Contessa slipped out, accompanied by Nick. I directed an icicle glare along the hall and pulled Bert rather quickly back to the ballroom. The music had stopped, and waiters were carrying around silver trays of drinks and hors d'oeuvres.

The eats had taken a serious downturn from the days of Lucullus. What was on the bread and crackers was mostly sardines and cheese. The wine was good, but it wasn't champagne. In a few minutes, Nick joined us.

"I see you and the Contessa hit it off pretty good," Bert said to him.

"She was showing me her art collection," Nick replied.

"Etchings, I assume?" I asked.

He ignored it. "She has half a dozen marvelous Impressionists. Mostly Monet, but one Renoir I've never seen before. She said it's been in the family for decades, and never shown." He snagged a glass of wine from a passing waiter and looked around the room. "Is our friend, Greenwood, here?" I guess he didn't want to say Boisvert in public, so translated it to English.

"No sign," I told him. "We haven't detected any French being spoken at all. Maybe if you put on your glasses you could help us look."

"You can't wear sunglasses at an evening party. I lost my clear ones."

I thought Bert had fainted. I was aware, from the corner of my eye, that he was sinking below my field of vision. "Bert, what's the matter? Are you sick? It's those sardines! They tasted awful."

"Must be Conan," Nick said in alarm, and looked all around.

Conan would have been easy to spot in a room of normal-sized people, even without glasses, though I was wearing mine. He wasn't there, but Bert had slunk to the ground and was duck-walking out of the room. Of course we followed him from behind, to conceal his ungainly exit.

"Maria," he gasped, and pulled himself upright when we reached the hall. "I've got to get out of here. I don't think she saw me."

"What would be she doing here?" I asked suspiciously.

"She works in a gallery. The Contessa'd know her," Bert said. "One of you guys find Nancy and let's split."

"I'll get her," I volunteered. I wanted to see Maria. I was curious to learn what kind of woman would appeal to a man like Conan. I pictured a voluptuous siren. "What's Maria wearing?"

"She had on a black dress, strapless."

I went back into the ballroom. There was only one young woman in a black strapless dress—it fit like wallpaper. She was only more or less in it, with a generous overflow at the top. An elderly man, sans ribbons, was patting her here and there and smiling lasciviously. Well he might. Maria had more curves than the Guggenheim Museum. Beside her, Nancy would look like a coatrack.

When I recovered from her extraordinary physique, I took a look at her face. My first thought was of a Raphael Madonna. That was the immediate, overall impression. She looked sweet and gentle. Then she turned and looked straight at me, and I saw the Madonna had brimstone in her eyes and a steely set of lips. She must have seen me with Bert. For a minute she looked me up and down. Her satisfied little smirk told me her opinion of me as possible competition. She walked away from her escort without a word, straight to me.

"Scusi," she said, "but you are American?"

"Yes."

"I think you are with Signor Garr?" Flames leapt in her dark eyes. Her voice was strident, like a fishwife in heat. Conan was the proper match for this woman. She looked capable of demolishing me—or him—with one hand. "Where is he?"

"I—he was—just around somewhere," I said vaguely.

She sneered and strode away, out the proper door to catch Bert. When I began looking around for Nancy, I happened to see the Contessa, standing on the sidelines. She was watching Maria with fixed interest. She glanced at me, and looked away quickly when she saw me staring at her. I searched till I found Nancy and beckoned her. She came right away.

"What's up?"

"Maria's here. She's gone after Bert."

"Maria, which one was she? No, don't tell me. She was the tart in the black dress—right?"

"That's her."

"She'll have a moustache by the time she's forty."

"I don't think anyone will notice."

We hurried out into the hallway. Maria was thrusting herself against Bert, and talking a mile a minute, in Italian, of course. Her white hands clutched his arms. Nick stood listening with an air of amused detachment, and began translating for us. "She says she's afraid of Luigi. She wants Bert to take her home."

"If she sets a foot in your car, I walk," Nancy announced.

"Bert's explaining that he came with a lady."

Maria flashed a dangerous eye at Nancy. I don't know about Nancy, but I trembled. She had the eye of an assassin.

"He's saying he'll call her tomorrow," Nick told us.

We watched as Bert tried to free himself from the prehensile young lady. I thought he might enjoy showing us how much Maria liked him, but he only looked trapped, and rather frightened. Of course he was thinking of Conan. At last he pulled free and ran, literally, to the front door. Maria cast a calculating look at Nick. I grabbed his arm and we followed Bert out.

Bert was at Nick's car, panting. "Wow! These signorinas!" He laughed nervously. "I thought she was going to wrestle me to the floor, right in the villa." He glanced around at the shadows, fearful that Conan was lurking nearby. "Unlock the car, Nick."

"It isn't locked."

"I can't get the door open."

Nick got in and punched it open from the inside. Bert was nearly inside before the door was open. "Let's blow this joint," he gasped.

The car coughed and spluttered for a minute, but finally moved.

CHAPTER 9

There was an air of constraint in the Alfa-Romeo as Nick flew us home. It started as soon as he grazed a Bentley trying to wiggle out of the parking area. Its origin was older. As far as I was concerned, it had started when Bert said, "He must have pulled the old 'he'd love to paint you' stunt." Nick's rendezvous with the Pasta Contessa didn't help, of course. Nancy and Bert were having words in the backseat as well.

"How was I supposed to know she'd be there?" I heard him say. Nancy's answer was a chilly silence.

In the front seat the conversation was, "If you'd buy some glasses you wouldn't hit so many cars."

"I didn't hit it. Our tires rubbed."

"Tires don't stick out. When cars sideswipe each other, it is not the tires that take the impact."

"My wheels were turned at a sharp angle. My tire grazed his."

"My God, and you men call women vain!" I said loftily, adjusting my glasses.

"It's not vanity!" he growled. "I've bought dozens of pairs of glasses. I just lose them. That's all. Anyway, I can see perfectly without them."

In the backseat, Nancy's silence had given way to strident snipes. "Oh sure, Bert. Luigi's chasing you all over Rome, beating the hell out of you because you held Maria's hand at a movie."

"Dates are taken seriously here. The girls are practically kept cloistered."

"Whereas in Troy, of course, we're all harlots! The bitch was laminated to that old man like wallpaper on a wall. Don't try to tell me she's fresh out of a convent."

"What did that sign say?" Nick shouted to the occupants in general.

"I thought you could see perfectly," I reminded him.

"It's dark, and we're going fast."

"Then slow down."

He stepped harder on the gas, till we were all being shaken like cocktails in a mixer. We turned a corner, with a quick thump-thump as he went up over the curb, then down again. A lamp stand missed us by millimeters, and not many millimeters either. "Oh jeez, you're lost again, Nick. This isn't the way home!" Bert called.

"We're not going home," Nick told him. "We're going to your apartment to get your car. One fight at a time is all I can handle when I'm driving. You drive Nancy home."

"I'd rather not be in a car alone with Mr. Garr, if you don't mind, Nick," Nancy said.

"She no fly," Bert said. "Rad's busted."

"I thought you were getting it fixed," Nick grouched. "You've had it parked for weeks."

"Damned rad. The guy was supposed to come and fix it up today. He promised it'll be ready by tomorrow. You can have Lana all to yourself after we get home, if that's what's bugging you."

"Yes, for as long as it takes a taxi to get to the house and take us to a hotel," I added.

"That's too long to suit me," Nick muttered under his breath. He leapt another curb. In the interest of getting home alive, we all stopped arguing. We proceeded in stony silence to Nick's driveway, where I opened my own door and we all went, Indian file, to the house. Nick unlocked the front door in silence. In silence we entered, one by one.

"A night cap, anyone?" Nick inquired in the cool accents of a host, determined to be civil while his guests behaved like yahoos. He looked more like a nobleman than anyone at the Contessa's party. I admired his style, even while hating him.

"What did you have in mind, Campari or cyanide?" I asked.

"Name your own poison."

"We'll be getting up very early to start phoning for buses and trains," I said loftily. "It's straight to bed for me. And in case you're not up yet when we leave in the morning, Nick, I want to thank you now for your hospitality." Neither of us mentioned calling a taxi, or removing immediately to a hotel.

"It was my pleasure." His black eyes skewered me. A muscle in his jaw quivered, but his nostrils didn't dilate. Nancy jumped in with her thanks. For a few minutes, it seemed rational intercourse (of the conversational type) might be re-established. Nancy talked to Nick; I talked to Bert, but after a moment both conversations fell to the ground, and Nancy and I went up to bed. Bert and Nick stayed below. Nick said something about finishing his Frageau, and Bert was going to make himself a sandwich.

In our room, Nancy threw her purse on the bed so hard it knocked a pillow on the floor. While I sat down and eased my aching toes out of the confines of tight sandals, she began pacing, throwing her arms around and enjoying a tantrum.

"Am I being unreasonable?" she demanded. "I mean tell me if I'm being unreasonable."

"You're being unreasonable. Bert didn't know Maria would be there. He went a mile out of his way trying to avoid her."

"I don't mean that! It's his stupid lies, letting on he never had anything to do with her except to take her to a movie, and that mob scene birthday party at her house."

"What's that got to do with you? It's ancient history. You haven't been exactly twiddling your thumbs the past few years."

"You're not *listening*, Lana. It's the lying. How can anyone establish a relationship if there's no trust? If he'd just come right out and say 'I had an affair with her,' that'd be it. I'd understand. The thing is, he's crazy about the girl. That's what's eating him inside. If it weren't for Luigi, he'd be married to her right now, this minute."

"He tried to avoid her tonight. Do you want the bathroom first?" I asked, hoping to derail her, and already regretting that I'd get stuck with her bathroom mess. Jealousy had had the undesirable effect of making Bert seem more appealing. That much was obvious.

She ranted on awhile longer about mutual trust and integrity, then said, "And what's with you and Nick? You seemed pretty touchy."

"He lied, too." She gave me an interested look, and I told her what Nick had said about wanting to paint my picture nude.

"What's wrong with that? He's an artist, Lana. They're like doctors where the naked body is concerned. To them it's just an arrangement of planes and curves and angles. You shouldn't take it so personally."

"Silly me. I feel taking off my clothes for a man is personal. Bert said he uses it as a ploy to get women."

"Men are bastards."

"Yes, even the ones with a full set of parents."

"Are we really leaving in the morning?"

"Yes. We'll have to send Nick some sort of present before we leave. Flowers or wine or something, to show our appreciation."

"You can't send flowers to a man. We'll never know what happened—about the Frageaus and everything."

"Maybe we'll read it in the papers."

"It'd be more fun to be here."

"Fun?"

"More exciting than being at home anyway. I wouldn't mind too much missing Salerno." Nancy was at the mirror, taking off her jewelry. She peered over her shoulder to see how I took to this idea.

I busied myself removing my pantyhose and examining my Band-Aids. They had stayed in place remarkably well. "I hope this doesn't turn into a corn. That's all I need."

"About Salerno . . . The thing is, I promised Bert I'd

move his car for him tomorrow. Before the fight, I promised. The American student he sublet his apartment to needs the parking space."

Talk about weak excuses. "How can you move a car with a busted rad?"

"His friend was supposed to have it fixed by tomorrow at ten."

"Friend—ha! He probably isn't even a mechanic. Besides, this is Italy. You know perfectly well the car won't be fixed. And anyway, what's the problem? He can park it here, hide it in the garage if he doesn't want Conan to know he's living here."

"He's afraid Luigi'll be waiting for him at the apartment. The man's an animal."

"Let Nick move it then."

"I said I would, and I don't want to break my word. Luigi wouldn't hurt a woman."

"No, but the traffic would. You must be crazy, offering to drive here."

"I happen to have a perfect driving record. I've never had an accident in ten years."

We weren't really arguing about her lame excuse of moving the car, but about staying on at Nick's. I didn't plan to give in on this one and said, "We might have time to move it before the bus leaves. We could park it at the bus terminal. That should confuse Conan."

"Yeah," she said, disappointed that I'd managed to find a way for her to keep her promise, and still leave. Now that I'd succeeded, I was none too happy about it myself.

Sleep was difficult with Nancy sniffling into her pillow, and a heaviness on my own heart. The interlude was over. Our romantic vacation would resume its unromantic tenor of bus, hotel, sightseeing, eating, hotel, bus, sightseeing. It was like putting down a book halfway through. We'd never know who dunnit, as it were. Maybe Nick would call from Boston when he went to visit his father at Christmas. Maybe.

Eventually we slept, and in the morning I woke early. Nancy was still sawing logs. She must have cried half the night, because she was usually up revoltingly early. Like any normal emotional coward, I waited till she was up and dressed before going downstairs, using the extra time to pack my suitcase. I needn't have bothered waiting. Nick was in his studio, working on the Frageau. Bert was at the table alone, looking down at the mouth.

"I called the bus and trains," he said with a quick dart of his eyes at Nancy. "Your best bet's the eleven-fifteen direct to Naples. You don't want to get on the local that stops at every chicken farm and olive tree."

"Then I'll be able to move your car before I leave," Nancy replied coolly. "If you'll give me the keys, I'll do it right after I pack. Lana suggested we leave it at the bus terminal."

"How do we get to the apartment, by taxi?" I asked.

"Nick'll drive you there," Bert said.

"He's had breakfast, has he?"

"All he could get down was coffee. Poor Nick." Bert's green eyes slid uncertainly in my direction. "You've been pretty tough on him, Lana. After all, you can't blame a guy for trying." I felt, however, that you could blame him for trying in such a shabby and unoriginal way. "Reminds me, he said to call him when you gals came down."

He got up and went to the studio. Nick came back with him, looking subdued and rather continental with a paisley scarf around his neck. Not stuck into the shirt like an ascot, but just tied with the ends out loose. He gazed into my eyes and said, *"Buon giorno, signorina."*

It was the first time he'd spoken Italian to me. I'd heard him speaking it to other people, but there was some seduction in hearing the intimate susurrus of the syllables, and seeing the apologetic gleam in his obsidian eyes. I said, "Hi."

"Any of that coffee left?"

I poured, and he sat beside me. "Want to see the Frageau? It's about finished. I did it in four hours. They used to take me weeks."

"Thanks, I'd love to. What are you planning to do with it?"

"Use it as a catalyst, and see if I can stir up some excitement."

"How?"

"I haven't decided yet. I have to do a quick aging job on it. It shouldn't look brand new. The acrylics dry very quickly. There are some Gauloises around here someplace. Smoke helps."

Over breakfast of fruit, coffee, and croissants, we talked about this safe subject, unwilling to shatter the fragile truce by discussing more meaningful matters. After breakfast, I went to the studio with Nick. The Frageau was on the easel, looking impressive but very new. It was a fairly complex expressionist thing, executed with a lot of verve and enthusiasm. I unwisely used the word Cubism. Nick looked offended.

"They were so studied! If Pollock slashed instead of dripped, he might have done something like this." The signature was copied from the "Frageau" in *Art World,* with a big, bold *F* in black, and the rest of the letters smaller.

"I didn't use much white. White looked too new," he explained, "but I always used some, so I put in these thin lines."

"You splattered this up in four hours, and some idiot's willing to pay you fifty thousand dollars for it. It just doesn't seem fair."

"It helps make up for all the hundreds of hours spent on works that didn't bring a penny. The irony is that I wanted money so badly when I was doing this sort of work, and never got it. I just wanted to impress my dad. Money was the only thing that would do it. An artist has to choose between two routes—being part of the establishment, or the loner. With my father's warnings of failure ringing in my ears, I studied the successful artists and decided this was what art patrons wanted. Well, they didn't—not then. So I left Paris and just did what *I* wanted to do. I ignored the art dealers, the galleries, all that. I worked alone, till a friend took one of my paintings to a gallery here in Rome. The dealer loved it, and placed four or five paintings with known collectors, but then he thought if I made my canvases a little darker, a little more in the Renaissance style . . ." He gave a rueful shake of his head.

"You mean—forgeries?"

"Oh no, just imitations. So I left him, but by that time I had a coterie of admirers. Then Bert came along, and with the intention of thumbing my nose at the establishment, I hired him as my agent. To my surprise and delight, he's a good one." I must have looked disbelieving, because he added, "We artists are expected to be a little outré, and besides, Bert—" He stopped and shrugged his shoulders.

I had a fair idea what had happened. He knew perfectly well Bert was scrounging for a living. He felt sorry for him, but didn't want to give charity. Bert had that ability of appealing to soft-hearted people. He was also a good scrounger, and had managed to sell the paintings. "I guess Bert must seem pretty outré to the art world."

"He adds a breath of fresh air. And of course the fact that he's a foreigner in Italy tends to—" He came to a sudden stop, not wanting to come right out and say that this helped hide Bert's blemishes.

He hurried on with a longish spiel. "I've gone from anonymity to the edge of making it big. I have a house, money in the bank. Like lots of artists, I've had to sell my watch or clothes or furniture to buy pigments. It's knowing that one day we might sell for a good price that gives us heart to go on. It applies to all the creative arts, I imagine. Music, writing, etc. It's the lure of major success that goads us on. And of course the impossibility of quitting," he added matter-of-factly. "Art is a mistress. Difficult, demanding, soul destroying when it goes wrong, but when it goes right, it's better than—" He stopped again. I mentally filled in the three letter S word. "No, Freud is dead," he said, apparently reading my mind. "It's heaven!"

"Ah, God has come back to life."

He turned the soft gleam of his black diamond eyes on me and said gently, "I have to believe in Him, since I've come to know you. What went wrong between us, Lana? Was it jealousy of the Contessa? Rosa's a happily married woman."

"You achieved a first-name basis, did you?"

"Yes, and that's all I achieved. I'm not a minuteman, you know. It was strictly business last night. We went to the party to see what we could discover. I discovered she's extremely eager to get a look at my early work. I wasn't trying to make her my mistress."

He put his arms around my waist and smiled tentatively. "It's you I want to make love with," he said. His arms tightened. His black silk head lowered, and his warm lips found mine.

I had often pictured kissing Nick. In my fantasies, it happened at night in some romantic spot with warm Italian zephyrs breathing over us. It must have been his terrace, because in my mind's eyes, that particular view of Rome spread below us. Yet it wasn't exactly his terrace. There was the gurgle of fountains that are so omnipresent in Rome.

It had never happened in a studio smelling of paints, in broad daylight, with the door open. Truth to tell, in the fantasy, there had been a little more persistence on his part. Now I seized his lips with an unmaidenly eagerness, and thrust my meager feminine allurements against his chest. The seduction of his caresses, especially the endearments murmured in Italian that were breathed into my ear between kisses, caused my innards to turn to warm zabaione. He used words like *bella, deliziosa, carissima.* And as his artistic fingers reached for my breasts, *stupendo,* which was a gross exaggeration. I nearly forgot the word "mistress." It was his using the word *letto* that brought it to mind. Rather similar to the French word for bed—*le lit.*

After a delightful wrestling match I disentangled myself from his clinging arms. "Bert says the bus leaves at eleven-fifteen."

"You're not leaving now!" It was a protesting howl of disbelief.

"No, not till eleven-fifteen. Well, I suppose we should leave by ten-fifteen, that will give us time to move Bert's car and make it to the bus station."

Astonishment blazed on his handsome face. "I'll take

you to the bus station. I'll move the car," he offered eagerly.

All this compliance was in the interest of arranging time for *letto*. As it also saved Nancy and me the hair-raising risk of driving in Italy, however, I accepted graciously. "Would you? Then we'll have time for another cup of coffee before we have to pack." He couldn't know I already had, and besides, Nancy hadn't. I headed for the door.

"But—" I heard the frustration in his voice, and kept on walking.

CHAPTER 10

While we had more coffee, Bert decided he'd drive down-town with us. Apparently he felt safe in a crowd, safer than being alone at the villa. "You can drop me off at the Quattrocento while you pick up my car and take the girls to the bus depot, Nick. I'll talk to Alberto, see if any of our French friends have shown up."

Nancy, who is often surprisingly capable of keeping her head while all about her have lost theirs, said, "No, you'll have to take Nick's car when we reach your apartment, Bert, or it will be left behind. The student needs the parking space, doesn't he?"

"Oh yeah. I forgot."

"Then you might as well take your own car," I suggested.

A confusing conversation ensued, in which the men discussed who would follow whom where, to ensure that neither of them had to walk a step. It was eventually worked out that Bert would pick up his own car and drive it to the Quattrocento while Nick took us to the bus stop. I kept wondering when we were going to find time to send Nick the wine. We'd have to do it from Salerno.

Nick said, "You stick around the gallery till I get there, Bert, and if Boisvert or his friend show, follow them."

"Roger."

In a sad and sentimental mood, Nancy and I wanted to say goodbye to Rome from Nick's terrace. After she had packed, we went out there, around to the side where the tiled roofs gleamed in the sunlight, their serenity punctuated with domes, campaniles, and spires, and the cars streamed down the hill. Nancy was blubbering into a Kleenex. My tears stayed in my throat, like a wet sponge. We didn't speak, but just looked and sighed.

After we had stored up memories for home, I said, "We'd better go."

The men were waiting at the bottom of the stairs with our luggage, which had grown into a small mountain. "We have a bit of a problemo, ladies," Bert pointed out. "We're never going to get all this gear into the Alfa-Romeo with four passengers."

I felt cheated. I was going to have to say goodbye to Nick here, our last moments together torn from us. "Right, we'd better call a taxi," I said, in a businesslike way.

"I could take one of you," Nick suggested, looking hopefully at me. "The taxi would be crowded, too."

"Nancy won't want to go alone," I pointed out.

Nick looked at me as if I'd struck him. "I'll call the taxi." He pronounced it *tassi*, which is the Italian word for it. It was his way of slurring his words that made his speech sound so romantic.

He called the taxi and we all waited, promising to write. Nick said he'd call me at Christmas from Boston, but he probably wouldn't. Bert said he'd be touching down in the good old U.S. of A. one of these days. Then the taxi came and we left, smiling determinedly till the door was slammed and we were off, smothered in luggage.

Neither Nancy nor I had much idea where the bus station was, but Nancy had an inkling the man was taking us the wrong way, through heavier traffic than necessary to slow us down, and increase the fare. I had put on my dark glasses to hide the moistness of my eyes, and let her worry about it. She kept looking out the window and complaining out loud. Suddenly she made a convulsive leap and shouted, "Stop! *Arretez*!"

"That's French," I told her.

"Stop! Didn't you see him?"

"Who?"

"Boisvert! That was him going into that hotel."

The driver squealed to a stop and poured a tirade of angry Italian over us.

"Quant'è la corsa?" Nancy asked, and started pulling bills out of her purse.

The driver told her a price that sounded grossly inordinate. She paid and we got out, pulling our suitcases after us. We stood in the middle of a so-so street, not a slum, but certainly not the Via Condotti.

"He went in there!" Nancy said, pointing to an old stone hotel. The sign above said Risorgimento, and it looked about that vintage, mid–nineteenth century, which is fairly modern for Italy.

"We're going to miss the bus to Naples."

We exchanged a broad grin. "Yeah," she said, and laughed. "We have to phone Nick. I hope they haven't left the house."

"They were going to do something about aging the Frageau before they left. I'll watch the hotel for Boisvert. You find a phone and call Nick."

"We'll check our bags at the Risorgimento," she said. "Boisvert doesn't know what we look like."

"They won't let us leave our bags if we don't hire a room."

Nancy stuck out her boobs and smiled. "Don't be silly."

With her few Italian phrases and her long eyelashes and cantilevered bra, she got our cases stowed safely behind the reception desk, and even had the clerk place the call for us. I listened while she hissed into the receiver, "Nick, it's me, Nancy. That Mr. Greenwood you're interested in . . . I found him for you."

Nick's voice sounded like the bark of a dog. She relayed her message, smiled sweetly at the clerk, and said, *"Grazie, signore."*

The clerk glowed with pleasure, and we left. "What'd Nick say?" I asked.

"He's coming right down."

"Boisvert will kill him!"

"He's bringing a gun. There are terrorists in Italy," she added, when my eyes bulged at the news that Nick owned a gun. "He says we should take a cab back to his place."

"Is Bert coming with him?"

"He didn't say."

"I'm not leaving here if Nick's going to see Boisvert alone."

"Of course we're not leaving, silly." We looked around for a sofa or coffee shop. "We'll go into the Garibaldi Room and have an espresso. If we sit near the door, we'll be able to see the lobby."

That's what we did. Before too long, a red streak outside the window told us the Alfa-Romeo had made it without its driver getting killed. We ran to the door and intercepted Nick.

"Didn't Bert come with you?" I asked.

"No."

"Why not?"

"He's aging the Frageau."

"You can't go up there alone."

He patted a bulge in his jacket pocket and grinned. "I'm carrying heat."

"You watch too many American movies."

"If you hear a shot, go start the engine. I might have to make a quick getaway." He uttered a low, excited laugh, and tossed the car keys on the table. "I'm parked right outside." In the no parking zone, no doubt. "I'll get Boisvert's room number at the desk."

He left, and I picked up the keys. I felt as if I was sitting on an atom bomb, and didn't know what to do. From our table we could see Nick go to the reception desk. The clerk was shaking his head. In a minute or so Nick was back. "Boisvert didn't use his own name. I don't know what room he's in. I'm going to ask around the maids for a Frenchman. The clerk just came on duty. He doesn't know, but some-body must." He left again.

"Bert should have come with him," Nancy said.

"I wonder why he didn't." I knew what Nancy was thinking. If Bert had been doing a little Frageau business with Boisvert on the side, he might have stayed home to notify Boisvert Nick was on his way. "I hope he didn't phone Boisvert and let him know Nick was coming!"

"Oh God! I'm going to phone Bert." Nancy jumped up and ran to the clerk. She was soon back. "Bert didn't answer," she said. Her face was chalky, and her eyes were glazed. "He's supposed to be aging the Frageau. Why didn't he answer? I've got to warn Nick."

"We'll both go."

"No, one of us better stay here. Nick told you to start the car in case of trouble."

"He wasn't serious—was he?"

"Now it's serious," Nancy said, and strode into the lobby, turning right at the desk, as Nick had.

I sat on alone, looking at a bitter cup of espresso and clenching the car keys in my fist. I should do something more—call the police maybe. Except that I might only succeed in getting Nick arrested. I knew he had a gun, but I didn't know Boisvert had. He had his henchman to do his shooting for him.

A few people straggled in and out of the hotel. I watched, in case I should spot Boisvert or his hired gun. A funny-looking man in a black beard and moustache with a Panama hat pulled low over his sunglasses caught my eye as he entered. He even walked funny, with his shoulders all hunched forward. It looked like a disguise, but the man was too small to be Boisvert, and too big to be his henchman. Probably just some roué keeping an assignation with a prostitute. It looked like that kind of hotel.

The man didn't stop at the reception desk, so he was apparently either a registered client or visiting a room whose number he already knew. Something about the man bothered me. I couldn't possibly know him. Had I seen him at the Quattrocento? At the Contessa's party? No, there hadn't been anyone there in run-down loafers. Oh my God! Bert Garr! What was he doing here? Had he phoned Boisvert, and arranged to come and help him take care of Nick?

I leapt up from my chair and pelted into the hall. He had

disappeared. There was a creaky old elevator with grillwork doors, but I decided to use the stairs. With my heart banging in my throat I ran up the wide, dusty stairway to the next floor. A couple of tourists, the woman in a blue dress and red face, the man in a white shirt and red face, stalked past, belching German. There was no one else in the corridor. I walked slowly down, listening at each doorway. I heard a couple of youngsters fighting with their mother in English, another German couple talking, and some gurgling, international lovemaking noises, but mostly all I heard was silence.

Back to the stairs and up to the next floor. Various activities were going forth in various languages, including maids making beds and flushing toilets, but there was nothing that sounded like Nick, or Bert, or Boisvert, or Nancy. There was just one more floor, and it was half empty, even at the height of the tourist season. Where had they all disappeared to? I took the elevator back downstairs and met Nancy, waiting in the lobby.

"Where did you go?" she demanded petulantly.

"Where did everybody go? Bert's here."

"No!"

I told her about the disguise. "Maybe he came to help Nick," she suggested hopefully.

"Why would he bother disguising himself from Nick? If he's been telling the truth, Boisvert doesn't know him. Obviously he was afraid Nick would see him. He came to help Boisvert."

"Honestly, Lana, I don't see why you're so negative about everything."

"You're the one that made me suspect him in the first place."

"Sure, of petty nickle and dime stuff. He'd never help Boisvert murder Nick."

"Then why were you so worried when he didn't answer the phone? Anyway he's here, and he's disappeared."

A waiter from the Garibaldi Room looked down the hall at us. "We didn't pay for our espresso," I reminded her. We went back to the table.

"I'm having a Campari and soda, even if it is morning," Nancy said. I nodded and she ordered two. When they arrived, she said, "I can't believe we're sitting here, drinking while Nick and Bert are . . . Oh what the hell *are* they doing anyway?"

Before long, Nick came back, looking crestfallen. "I can't find him," he admitted. "He must be booked in here. I'll have to do a stakeout."

"Bert's here," I announced.

"He came to help you," Nancy added firmly.

Nick grinned. "Good old Bert. I knew he wouldn't be able to keep away. Where is he?"

"Search me. He came in fifteen minutes ago." I described the disguise.

"His Toulouse-Lautrec outfit. He wore it to a masquerade party at my place last year."

To my shame, my first reaction was jealousy of that party, and his escort. I'd never been to a masquerade party. Why were we so dull in Troy? Then it occurred to me that Bert had purposely worn a disguise that Nick recognized, and I felt a wave of relief. Almost immediately the realization followed that he must be hiding from Boisvert, and that meant Boisvert would recognize him. So they had had doings. I gave Nancy a piercing look, suggesting she should drop a few hints about Bert's other possible reason for being here.

She lifted her chin and said, "Just like Bert. He wouldn't leave you in the lurch."

"I hope he took the Frageau out of the oven before he left," Nick said.

"He'll probably go by the door soon," Nancy said firmly. "Then we'll all decide what to do."

"Why don't you two take your luggage back to the house and do some sightseeing, or shopping?" Nick suggested.

The "take your luggage back to the house" was slipped in unobtrusively. He looked at me, with a smile in his eyes.

I said, "The tour must be wondering what happened to us."

"I'll phone Ron later this morning," Nancy said. "We'll join the tour in Salerno."

Nick glanced out the window and said, "Oh cripes."

We followed the line of his gaze. The Contessa was just climbing out of a white Bentley, wearing her yellow tinted shades again, and looking like a million dollars. She disappeared, and in a minute she was at the lobby. She looked into the Garibaldi Room and saw us. She did a quick double take but recovered quickly, like a lady who was accustomed to unpleasant surprises. Possibly even a crook? Nick lifted his hand and waved, and she came in, smiling.

"Niccolò!" She kissed him, just left of center on the lips. A peck on the cheek was the more conventional Latin greeting. A short spate of Italian ensued between them. I made use of it to admire her dress, a mint green linen today, with the same array of tinkling bracelets and green snake-skin sandals. And still no blisters adorned her slender feet. How did she walk on those stilts? She said a few words to us, and left.

"She was just driving by and stopped to pick up some matches," Nick explained. "Terrible habit, smoking." His intelligent eyes told his opinion of that excuse.

"A funny place for her to happen to be driving by," I said. "Even funnier that her car doesn't have a lighter."

"Funniest of all, she doesn't smoke," Nancy added.

"I never have seen her smoke, now that you mention it," Nick said. "So she knows Boisvert. Why else would she be here?"

Nancy erupted into raucous laughter as she does when her nerves have had more than enough. "She must have been ready to crown us when she saw us sitting here."

Nick beckoned for the bill. "We better scram. She'll call Boisvert. I'd rather not find a bomb under my hood."

"We can't leave Bert here alone!" Nancy exclaimed.

"He probably slipped out some back door ages ago," Nick said. "He'll be waiting for us at the villa, wearing his stupid-innocent face."

"But Boisvert might check out," I said.

"It doesn't matter now. We know where Rosa lives, and they'll be getting together," Nick said, with one of his lazy, langorous smiles.

CHAPTER 11

We had some good luck, and some bad. The good luck was that the car wasn't bombed, nobody followed us, and Nick didn't hit anything—except the pillar when he pulled into the driveway at his house, and that was only a light tap. You could hardly see the new dent in the fender. The bad news was that Bert wasn't at the villa. Oh, and Nick considered it good news that Bert had remembered to take the Frageau out of the oven. Not that anything would have happened to it at one hundred degrees Farenheit, and with the oven door open. Bert had forgotten to turn off the oven. Nick lit four Gauloises and propped them on a plate with the smoke wafting toward the painting. We all held our noses and looked at this bizarre scene for about two minutes.

Nancy said, "He must still be at the hotel."

"Maybe we should go back," I suggested. "We left our luggage there."

Nick said, "Right, we'll go back."

He changed his shirt to a red and white Hawaiian print, put on his dark glasses, a camera over his shoulder, and a silly-looking white cotton hat turned down all around. "I'm disguising myself," he explained.

"As who, Don Ho?" I asked.

"As a tourist, in case Rosa reported me to Boisvert."

"I'm glad you're not trying to look inconspicuous."

"I hoped it might blind him."

"Works for me." I put on my shades, too, and we all left.

Nick parked a block away in a parking lot with an attendant, to prevent anyone from putting a bomb under his car. We walked past the hotel on the far side of the street. "There's a terrace outside!" I exclaimed, pointing.

"That's where they usually put them," Nancy said. She was still ticked off with me for not trusting Bert. "We wouldn't be able to see the lobby if we sat there."

"We're not particularly interested in the lobby," Nick said, and led us through a gate to the terrace. "You girls order something and I'll take a run inside."

"Do they sell lollipops?" I inquired. He gave me a wary look. "In future we'd both appreciate it if you didn't call us girls. We teach girls and boys."

His wariness turned to frustration. "The last time I called a girl a lady, she told me lady was a four letter word."

"So's a girl."

"What do you—female people—want to be called?"

"Woman is a nice, safe five letter word."

"So's b—" He bit back the *b* word, and muttered something in Italian, no doubt profane, into his collar. Before he left, our waiter came bustling up wearing a black beard and moustache, a short white jacket and run-down Gucci loafers.

"Bert! What are you doing here?" Nancy asked.

"The noon shift. Tables one to nine," he said out of the side of his moustache, handing us menus. "Stay clear of the pasta. They're reheating yesterday's. Looks like a tub of albino worms." Ugh!

"You mean you're working?" Nancy inquired.

"Read my lips."

"Read them? I can't even see them."

"I'm doing the noon shift. They're short-staffed, begging for help. I stumbled into the kitchen by mistake. They stuck this dumb short coat on me, and here I am. The tips are terrific, especially the Americans. Know how you tell a European from a canoe? The Europeans don't tip. And before you call me a racist, I want you to know I heard that one from a wop."

"I always tip!" Nick protested.

"Nothing personal, old buddy. And to prove I'm not a racist, I've got another one," Bert continued. "How do you tell an American from a rowboat?"

"I personally never had any trouble telling them apart," Nancy said.

"Boy, you guys sure know how to wreck a joke. If I said 'knock-knock' you wouldn't know enough to ask 'Who's there?' "

"All right, Bert. How do you tell the difference between an American and a rowboat?" Nick asked.

"The rowboat has both oars in the water," Bert said, and looked expectantly for applause.

"Now that you've insulted the western hemisphere, I have a question for you," Nick said. "Any sign of Mr. Greenwood or his associates?"

Bert frowned. "That's not a riddle—is it?"

"No, Bert. It's a question. Party time's over."

"Oh, you mean Boisvert. Not so far. The guys at table seven are parlaying français. Why don't I sit you next to them? You never know, they might have met our other French friends. *Oiseaux* of a feather, if you get my drift. They might let something slip."

We removed to table eight, across from two not uninteresting Frenchmen. They were younger than Boisvert's man, and more handsome.

Bert drew out his little pad and pen. "A Campari for starters, folks?"

"It's nearly noon. Let's eat," Nancy suggested.

We ordered the fruit plate with cottage cheese. Bert left, and I leaned an ear toward the next table and translated for the others. "There's either a rooster or a cockroach in their room," I said. "Or possibly a boiled egg. I'm not sure whether the word was *coq*, or *coque*, or *coquerelle*."

"Could that be Boisvert?" Nancy asked.

"I don't think so. He stepped on it. Must have been a cockroach. *Une jolie petite fille* told the one in blue where to go for a good time." Nick's interest perked up. "Unfortunately I couldn't make out the answer," I told him.

One of the Frenchmen wore a blue jacket, the other a

white shirt. The one in the white shirt was more handsome. He was soon sliding dark, hopeful glances at Nancy. "Smile at him," I told her. "Maybe you can get him talking."

She turned her head and batted her long lashes. The man turned his chair at forty-five degrees from the table, giving him a view of her body profile. She smiled shyly at him. "He's afraid I'm with you, Nick," she said. "Put your arm around Lana's shoulders."

Nick complied, in his own Latin way. "The shoulder's the part that sticks out at the sides, Nick. Not the front." I lifted his dangling fingers from my breast.

The Frenchman raised his glass in a salute to Nancy. She coyly turned away, but with an encouraging peep over her shoulder. Bert came back with our lunch. Three-quarters of the "fresh" fruit was straight out of a can. The "fresh" grapes were turning brown around the stem. The cottage cheese was sour, and the buns were the same consistency as the cobblestones underfoot. Not having to eat left Nancy more time for flirtation. Within two minutes, verbal contact had been established.

In a mixture of French, English, and a few stray words of Italian, introductions were made. Over coffee, the Frenchmen, Claude (handsome, white shirt) and Réné (so-so, blue suit), joined us. They were civil servants on holiday from Rouen. Usually they went to Germany, but this year they came to Italy instead. They seemed innocent, but I decided to add a catalyst of my own to the conversation.

"I teach Art in the States," Nancy smiled. "And my friend—" She turned to me.

I stretched my hand out to Claude and said, "Ms. Frageau. I'm an artist."

Claude gulped and his head swiveled to Réné. "But you're a woman!" They exchanged a startled look that held a question. Nick, Nancy, and I did likewise.

Réné recovered before his friend. "Are you also from America, Miss Frageau?" he asked.

"Yes, from Boston, but I lived for a few years in Paris before coming to Rome," I said, in case they knew where

Frageau-Hansen was born. I said it in French to substantiate the lie.

The atmosphere had become noticeably tense. Not even Nancy's fluttering lashes and smiles and deep inhalations that stretched her blouse to interesting proportions could detain them for long. They rose like twin puppets, shook our hands, said it had been *charmant* to meet us, threw some bills on the table, and took off like a pair of darts.

"I'll follow them," Nick said, and strode swiftly after them. They were all three running when we spotted them over the fence, hustling down the street. The blur of red, white, and blue looked like the American flag in a high storm.

"Why did you say that?" Nancy demanded.

"What did we have to lose? I wanted to see their reaction. Well, we saw it. They know I'm not Frageau. They know Frageau's a man. 'But you're a woman!' Claude said. Did Boisvert bring a whole *army* over here to kill Nick? He had one man at the gallery, now these two."

Bert noticed Nick had left and came to our table. "What's up?" he asked, moustache twitching.

"Do you happen to know if those Frenchmen are registered here at the Risorgimento, or were they drop-ins?" I asked.

"They came through the gate. That usually means they're drop-ins. Where's Nick gone? Was it just nature calling or—"

"He's chasing them," I said, and told him why.

He scratched his head, picked up the money from their table, pocketed two bills, and said, "Anything for dessert? The spumoni's safe. Nobody's complained about it yet."

"We might as well," Nancy said. "This is as good a place to wait for Nick as any."

We ordered spumoni. It seemed we were always sitting around like the chorus in a Greek tragedy, waiting and talking while the excitement occurred elsewhere. Bert was a little nervous; he kept looking over his shoulder and out into the street. Since Nick wasn't here, it was a good chance for Nancy to quiz him. He went for the spumoni, and I said,

"Why don't you ask Bert why he's dressed in that ridiculous disguise? You haven't forgotten our suspicion? He might be hanging around here, waiting for a word with Boisvert."

She gave me a dirty look. When he came back, she said, "You didn't tell us why you're wearing that wig, Bert."

"Why do you think? My rear end's up for grabs if Conan spots me. He might have heard I saw Maria at Lingini's last night." He didn't turn red.

Nancy was satisfied with this half explanation. I wasn't, but I'm not much good at direct confrontation. I had to steel myself to ask, and when I did, it came out more harshly than I had intended. "Were you selling Nick's old Paris paintings behind his back, Bert? Do you know Boisvert?"

"What?" He was genuinely confused. He was even too confused to be angry yet. It was Nancy that went for my throat, and she was the one who put the idea in my head in the first place.

"Nick trusts Bert implicitly. I don't see that it's your place to question him." She fluffed her blond locks over her shoulder and glared.

"Those two expressionist paintings disappeared. Bert had them," I reminded her.

"I didn't have them," Bert said. "Nick thinks I had them. Last time I saw them, they were in his studio. The guy that spiked our booze must have got them. Why else did he want us out of commission?"

He still wasn't red. I grudgingly admitted Bert was innocent. It finally dawned on him that his honor had been impugned. He put one hand on his hip, gave me a disparaging look and said, "Pshaw," or something like that. "Thanks for the vote of confidence, Lana. With friends like you, a guy doesn't need enemies."

"Just checking. I'm sorry, Bert."

"Aaah," he batted my hand forgivingly. "I know what my reputation is in Troy. It's the old Treasurer of the Student Council thing that's bugging you, right?"

I felt humbled at his forgiving so quickly, and easily. "Well . . ."

"It ain't easy being one of the gang when you don't have

an allowance. I delivered papers, did errands—for your Dad's drug store, among others. Did you ever hear of me rifling the till? No. My old man always had his hand out for any dough I made. He drank, you know. So I shaved two cents from the Student Council fund to take a girl to the Christmas Prom. Big deal. The money was for the students, right? Well, I was a student."

"You don't have to explain, Bert," I said, feeling like one and a half cents. I thought of that sign in his kitchen, "The hardest thing about becoming a millionaire is thinking you can do it." Poverty and ambition are a hard mix. "I'm sorry."

"Why do you think I was so anxious to get out of Troy? My name's mud there. As soon as my mom died, I split. I only stayed for her sake."

"Don't be silly. Everybody's forgotten about that," I assured him.

"Except you," he said. My value plunged to one cent. "My nose is clean here. Don't crap on my parade by telling Nick, okay?" I nodded. "Now eat your ice cream before it melts." He left.

Nancy glared at me as if I were a child murderer, and I felt a bit like one. "You're the one that suggested it!" I growled.

"You really hurt his feelings, Lana."

"I know, and I feel awful. I didn't know his dad drank." Not that this excused him entirely, but it was certainly an extenuating circumstance that bore consideration.

"You never really knew Bert," she said stiffly. "I knew his dad was a drinker. He gave the family an awful time, but Bert never complained. Not once. I wonder who it was Bert wanted to take out when he took the money from the Student Council. I bet it was Mary Livingstone."

"I don't know. Were you really engaged to him?"

"Oh Lana, he was so miserable when his mother was dying. Mom and I used to go over to help them out a bit. He cried, Lana, like a little boy. My heart just went out to him. He's sensitive, beneath that tough shell. He really loved his mother. His father was so mean—the drink, of course. Bert said he couldn't live with his dad, and when he asked me to go away with him—it was partly pity, but he really *is* a nice guy."

I felt worse than a child molester. My childhood had been so idyllic, I never even thought of such things as abused kids. Poor Bert. And I had never been nice to him. I was a smug, self-satisfied jerk. We finished our spumoni in silence. I left a huge tip, because I felt so guilty. Nancy took up some of the bills and handed them back. "Don't add insult to injury," she said.

I accepted the money humbly, feeling like an ugly American, trying to buy goodwill with cash. "What should we do now?"

"Bert's keeping an eye on things here. Let's get a taxi and take our luggage back to Nick's."

That's what we did. I checked the Frageau. The Gauloises had gone out, but the painting had lost its sheen of newness. Nancy phoned Ron in Salerno and left a vague message that we'd join them later, before they left Italy. We went out on the terrace to wait.

"Our tour colleagues will think we're shacked up with some men here in Rome," she said.

"We'll feel stupid when we join them. Imagine the smirks and comments."

"And the jealousy." She laughed.

We discussed putting on our bathing suits as the terrace was quite private. Before we got around to it, the Alfa-Romeo came streaking into the driveway and Nick got out. Nancy gave me another of her coy looks and said, "I'll leave you two alone a minute." I ran into the house.

"Did you find Boisvert?" I asked, scouring him for signs of lacerations or contusions. He was all in one undamaged piece, but he'd lost his hat.

"No, but I caught Claude and Réné. They're French cops. They're chasing Boisvert, too."

"Did you tell them he's at the Risorgimento?"

"They had already followed him there. They think he spotted them and slipped out the back way. That's why we couldn't find him. They're staying at the Santa Vittoria.

That's where I caught up with them. I'm supposed to phone them if I find Boisvert."

"Why are they after him?"

We sat on the sofa and Nick told me their conversation. "It has to do with Frageau. It *is* a made-up name, but there's a corpse of one Edouard Fargé in Paris who comes into the story as well. He drowned a year after I came to Italy. Boisvert claimed the body, identified it as Paul Frageau, and paid for the burial. The way we figure it, Boisvert got to examining the paintings I had left behind with him and decided that with a romantic story to get people interested, he might turn a few thousand francs on them. He figured enough time had passed that anyone who knew me had forgotten the kind of painting I did. So he cut off my signature, added Frageau's and held a posthumous exhibition for the drowned artist. His death was called suicide, due to public apathy regarding the young man's art. If you play it right, that old chestnut still brings in a few guilt-ridden collectors."

"Bert was right about that."

"More or less. One of them—Pierre Duplessis—liked my stuff and bought a painting. He showed it to his friends, including Georges St. Felix, and before too long, Boisvert had a hit on his hands. The price shot up. Unfortunately, it involved some publicity as well—just articles in local publications in Paris first—that was safe enough since I was in Italy. Then eventually the article appeared in *Art World*. Boisvert knew I'd see it. He must have been worried sick. But that wasn't the greatest of his worries. He had Edouard Fargé's father to worry about as well."

"That's the young man who drowned?"

"Exactly. After Edouard had been missing for a few weeks, his father became worried. Edouard was a no-good layabout, as far as I can make out. A spoiled rich kid who spurned his bourgeois family, but lived off them. His father gave him an allowance that let him set up a studio, but he spent most of his time and money doing various illegal chemicals. The father went looking at the house where Edouard lived, and was told his son had disappeared. Just walked out one day and never came back. So he began checking police records, morgues, etc., and decided that the body claimed by Boisvert as Frageau was actually his son."

"The body wouldn't still be in the morgue, though."

"Oh no, he had the body exhumed and identified Edouard by dental records and things. He went to Boisvert; Boisvert denied it, of course. There were lengthy legal discussions—France is riddled with red tape. Fargé was trying to get Boisvert indicted, if not for murder, at least for complicity in something illegal. Fargé thinks—or he's pretending he thinks—his son actually did my paintings, and is threatening to sue Boisvert for the money. It amounts to a quite a bit by now. Boisvert confessed the whole thing to Fargé—sort of. Except that he didn't identify Frageau as Niccolò Hansen. He just said Frageau had disappeared, but was still alive. He said he's looking for Frageau to give him the money. You can laugh at that one. He knows exactly where I am. He's just trying to keep Fargé's hands off the dough."

"Did he give Fargé any excuse for letting on you were dead, and claiming Edouard's body as yours?"

"Oh sure, the old dead artist stunt, as Bert calls it. He explained to Fargé that a dead artist's work is worth more, and since no one had claimed Edouard's body, he decided to pretend it was mine—Frageau's that is."

"So why did the police run when I announced I was Frageau? Wouldn't it have been more natural for them to question me?"

Nick riffled his fingers through his hair, thinking. "They knew Frageau was supposed to be a man."

"That should have made them all the more curious."

"I was so busy following their story that I didn't have much time to think." I gave him a withering stare. "They kept interrupting each other, too, and asking me questions. I was a little confused."

"So I gather."

"They did ask who you really are."

"This is a crock, Nick. According to that story, Boisvert should be trying to find you, and keep you alive, shouldn't he, to corroborate that the paintings don't belong to Fargé? Why is he having someone shoot at you?"

"But if he 'finds' me, he'll have to pay up. If Boisvert did manage to steal the two abstract paintings from my studio . . . He could keep the money himself, I suppose." He scratched his cheek doubtfully. "You're right. It's a crock. I'm no good at analysis. My talent is for creating things, not figuring them out."

"Boisvert couldn't keep the money if Fargé has anything to say about it. He needs you to prove you painted them. And what about the Contessa? Did you ask them about her being there?"

"They don't know Rosa at all." I gave another of my withering looks.

After a little more head rubbing, Nick said, "Maybe I'd better call Claude and check up on a few points." I went with him into the studio.

The conversation was in Italian, but I got the gist of it even before Nick hung up and said sheepishly, "They're not registered at the Santa Vittoria. Never were. They're con men."

"Weren't you in their room?"

"No, we talked in the bar. They were very generous with the vino, too. They conned me. Dammit! I should have smelled a rat. They're not policemen." He looked at me warily, waiting for a tirade.

"You should have been a rat, like them."

"I thought you thought I was."

Nancy appeared at the door. "Time's up," she called. "Am I interrupting anything?"

Nick was just starting to repeat his story when the motorcycle pulled into the driveway. He waited till Bert came in, so he'd only have to tell it once more.

Bert was smiling from ear to ear. He pulled bills out of his pockets and tossed them up over his head. "I'm rich!" he said. "Boy, this waitering is the racket. I'm going to try for one of the decent hotels. So what's shaking on the home front?"

"Pull up a chair," Nick said. "This'll take awhile."

"In that case I'll grab a beer and take off my shoes. My feet are killing me."

We all got a beer and went to the terrace. Nick told the story again.

"The sum and total of it is, you dropped the ball, Nick," Bert said. "We'll all have to put on our dunce caps and see if we can figure this out."

"That's thinking caps, Bert," Nancy pointed out.

"Whatever."

CHAPTER 12

"If those two guys aren't from the French Sureté, who are they?" Bert asked. "That, to quote the Bard, is the question."

"Boisvert's pals are the answer," Nancy said. "And they wouldn't be just ordinary cops. They'd be Interpol, wouldn't they?"

Nick looked interested. "They mentioned the Art and Fraud Squad. That's Interpol. So maybe Interpol's investigating Bosivert, if Fargé is kicking up a dust in Paris. They might be doing a quick scan of other countries, trying to find Frageau. But if Claude and Réné are Interpol, they'd want me to work with them. They wouldn't have any reason to lie to me and give me the wrong address. It might explain where their story came from though, if they've found out Interpol is in Rome. They had to say something to appease me, and claimed to be agents."

"And you believed it," Bert said, with a disparaging wag of his head. "How'd you like to buy the Colosseum, Nick? I can get if for you wholesale. You shouldn't be allowed to leave home alone."

Nick looked at me. "There, he saved you the bother of saying it."

"On the doubtful theory that there's an Interpol agent or agents in Rome, who do you figure it could be?" I asked. "We can eliminate Boisvert and his crooked-nose friend who broke in here and later shot at us. Réné and Claude aren't legit."

"I think we can assume anybody who keeps trying to avoid us, or taking potshots, is not Interpol," he said.

"That's sure not their MO," Bert told us.

"What would their MO be, Bert?" Nancy asked.

"Hey, I'm just a layman. Why ask me?"

I said, "Who else is left?"

"There's Conan and Maria," Nancy said doubtfully. "*They* certainly aren't trying to avoid Bert. But French agents wouldn't be Italian."

"Their hobby wouldn't be breaking men's bones," Bert added. "That's my purely personal problem. It has nothing to do with Nick. *Cherchez la femme*—or should I say *signora*? All we have left is the Contessa. No, dammit, she's Italian, too."

"Interpol's international," I reminded them. "Maybe she's working with the French."

"With those fingernails?" Nancy asked.

It sounds irrelevant, but as a symbol of the lady and her lifestyle, it didn't sound as stupid as it should have. Bert had mentioned she was the social lioness of Rome. I couldn't see her involved in police work, in her elegant shifts and snakeskin sandals. A beautiful young lady, married to an aging nobleman wasn't likely to risk her body working for the police.

"There isn't anyone else," Bert said, "not on our list of dramatis personae. And if Interpol's here, why didn't they contact Nick? What we have here, folks, is neither fish, fowl, nor good red meat. It's a red herring. Speaking of which, is anybody hungry? Lunch was a non-event."

"Let's eat in so we don't have to tackle the traffic," Nick said. "Lana, would you mind giving me a hand?"

The terrace was so beautiful I left it reluctantly. "What did you have in mind?" I asked, as we went to the kitchen. "For dinner, I mean," I added hastily. His black eyes were casting a sultry gaze on me, and his lazy smile suggested delightful non-cooking activities.

"Spaghetti, but not with meat balls. We'll make it *alla carbonara*. The only meat I have left is bacon."

"We're eating you out of house and home!"

"And jeering me out of my self-respect. I feel like such a dope, being outsmarted by those two fakers."

"It was the wine," I said forgivingly.

"Now you're thinking I'm a wino!"

"You're too upset to cook. Let me take you and Bert out to dinner tonight, Nick."

"We'll see. For now, you can earn your keep. Be my sous chef and toss a salad while the master cooks."

"Yes, master."

It was fun watching Nick cook. He certainly knew his way around a kitchen. And what a kitchen it was. Enough to make you want to buy an apron. The pots all gleamed. Funny little cooking tools hung on a pegboard, some of them I'd never seen before. He opened a bottle of red wine and we drank as we worked. He put on a huge copper pot of water to boil for the pasta, fried bacon and sauteed garlic and pimentos while I prepared the salad.

"The peppers are my own addition," he explained. "I put them in for eye appeal."

"That'd be the artist coming out in you."

He cocked his head and examined the pan. "Don't the red and green look pretty?"

"Like Christmas in July." I grated the pecorino cheese.

"I like pecorino romano best," he explained. It was a hard cheese, the color of straw with a black rind that I thought should be removed. "Leave it on. It adds a certain *je ne sais quoi* to the dish."

"I think I prefer to know what I'm eating. Black specks in my food put me off."

He shrugged. "As long as they don't have wings."

The aromas floating around the small room set my stomach grumbling in appreciation. Nick beat the eggs till they were silky, then he tasted the pasta and put a string in my mouth, gazing at me as we chewed. "What do you think?" I felt like the woman in *Tom Jones*, eating chicken while passion simmered.

"I'd say it needs two more minutes. It's still hard in the middle."

"Americans over-cook pasta. It shouldn't be mushy. I'll give it one minute."

I escaped and set the table. Nick was an inventive cook. On various trips to the kitchen I saw him regarding the earthenware crock of black olives, marinating in olive oil. He popped one into his mouth, then picked up a handful and tossed them in with the spaghetti before he added the eggs, so I added a few to my salad. He picked a piece of fresh oregano from a pot growing on his windowsill, stripped the leaves in one smooth motion, put one in his mouth and sprinkled the rest on top of my salad. On another trip he was removing a long, thin loaf of bread from the oven, where he had put it to warm. He even heated the plates—did it all so gracefully and easily, with none of the reeling pandemonium that occurred when I was in a kitchen alone.

Within twenty minutes we were all sitting around a table laden with the feast. "What did I tell you?" Bert said, as proud as if he'd done the cooking himself. "Didn't I say Nick was a great chef? *Numero uno*. Look out, Julia Child."

"This is *fabulous*," Nancy exclaimed. "I have to get the recipe for this, Nick. Is it hard to make?" He told her the ingredients. "But how much garlic?"

"Just a little—five or six buds."

"That much? It doesn't taste that strong."

"Don't squeeze them, just slice."

"And how much pecorino?"

"You don't measure," he said, surprised. "Just enough to make it taste right." His hands fanned the air, shoulders shrugging.

As we lingered over coffee, our talk turned inevitably to "the case." A summer storm had blown up suddenly, and we stayed at the table to talk, nibbling grapes and melon slices, with the wine lending a warm glow, and the flickering candles casting romantic shadows. Rain beat against the windows, and ran in tears down the glass. It only lasted ten minutes. I didn't ever want to leave Rome. I didn't want to leave the villa. I wanted to be Nick's sous chef forever. I wanted to learn to cook, Italian, style, with fresh herbs and funny cheeses, and black flecks in my food. Nick's jet hair and ruddy complexion were enhanced by the shadows. Even Bert looked good, and Nancy had a dreamy air about her. I wondered how I looked, since Nick's eyes were often on me, studying me with disturbing intimacy.

"This visit could have been a hell of a lot of fun if it weren't for Conan," Bert said. "Why did he introduce Maria to me in the first place, if he's so crazy about her?"

This surprised me. "Did he actually introduce you?"

"Sure. She works at the Minosi Gallery. He's the one who told me I should check it out. He owns a piece of it, maybe the whole thing. It's a small place."

"Where'd you meet him?"

"I met him a year ago, at Nick's exhibition. The gorilla's interested in art, believe it or not. Strange but true. He's the one that took me to the Minosi. Maria was all over me like snow in a blizzard. Make that sweat in the tropics."

"Let's stick with snow."

"He didn't seem to mind then," Bert said. "In fact, I got the idea he was encouraging her. Probably thought I was a rich American. Boy, did they get the wrong number! Maybe they weren't engaged yet. I was going with another girl at the time. I didn't call Maria. All she wanted from me was to put Nick's works in her gallery. The place is a two-bit affair. Nothing in the shop sold for more than five hundred bucks. I said thanks, but no thanks. Forgot all about her. Then about a month ago, we met again, in the Subura where I live. We went out a couple of times. That Sunday dinner with the family did it for me. Exitville. *Arrivederci,* Maria. These Italian girls get too serious too fast."

"It's odd she invited you home," Nick said. "Romans guard their homes jealously. If they want to be sociable, they take you to a restaurant. Home is for family and very close friends."

"The lady planned to make me part of the family, definitely," Bert said.

"When did Conan start chasing you?" I asked, sensing

something interesting here, because Maria did know the Contessa, who had been at the Risorgimento looking for, or meeting, Boisvert.

"Strangely enough, he didn't go after my hide till I had dropped her. It was all over between us, finis, but try telling him that."

"So Conan and Maria are interested in Nick's works, too," I said musingly.

Nick lifted his eyebrows. "They didn't happen to ask after any of my earlier works?"

"You got me there," Bert said. "It was a year ago, more or less, that they mentioned you. The second time around, it wasn't art we talked about. I don't think you came up at all, Nick. Maria met me, accidentally on purpose, if you know what I mean, at a little café in the Subura that I go to. She followed me there. To put it bluntly, the lady wanted my bod." He smiled complacently.

"What does Conan say when he's beating you up?" I asked.

"Italian cuss words mostly. He suggested I perform unspeakable acts on myself. He says in Italy women aren't seduced and abandoned. I've disgraced her. We haven't even—" he looked uncertainly at Nancy. "Really! Nothing happened. He says things like 'If you aren't going to marry Maria, keep away from her, or I'll rip out your guts and wrap them around your throat.' Stuff like that, with liberal swearing."

Nancy peered at him suspiciously. "I thought he was telling you to keep away from her. It sounds to me as if he's trying to coerce you into marrying her."

"He's got the wrong man. No gold bands for this bozo—and Maria, I mean." They exchanged a long, meaningful look. Lord, was Nancy thinking of marrying him? A whole future of having to be nice to Bert flashed in front of my eyes. I'd have to be their bridesmaid, godmother for their children. For as long as I lived, Bert Garr would be a part of my life. Then I remembered his awful childhood, and felt a wave of remorse. I looked toward Nick.

He wore a sly, considering face. "If you were an Italian

gentleman, Bert, you'd do the right thing by the lady. Thanks to you, Maria's lost Conan. He's trying to force you back to her."

"Sure, he's seen the family at the trough and wants out. Can't say I blame him, but he can get himself another fall guy. I'm no Italian gentleman. All I did with Maria was take her to a couple of movies and visit her family. Period."

"But visiting the family is such a serious step here," Nick insisted. "A forerunner to the betrothal."

Nancy took umbrage. "She was throwing herself at a rich old man at Lingini's party last night. She's no innocent young girl. Bert doesn't have to marry her just because Conan wants out. Why does he want you to, anyway?" she demanded, turning to Bert. "It's not as if you're rich. Have you been bragging to her, Bert?"

"No way," he said automatically, but a sudden puckering of his forehead intimated that he had. "Maybe he's got her pregnant."

"She certainly didn't look it last night in that black dress," I reminded them.

Nick's long, El Greco fingers began beating a tattoo on the table. His mind had wandered away from us. I knew by the faraway look in his eyes that he was conjuring with the case. "No, it's too late tonight," he mumbled into his glass.

"Too late for what?" I prodded.

"I think we should offer the Frageau to the Minosi Gallery," he said, with a diabolical grin.

"What about Lingini?" Bert demanded. "I practically told her she could have it."

"She can have it, if she likes it," Nick pointed out. "The Minosi will only exhibit it and sell it. Give other possible buyers a chance to bid. I'll insist they put it in the window."

Bert shook his head. "All this Conan-Maria business doesn't have anything to do with the painting. He wants to dump Maria and he's trying to put the blocks to me to take her off his hands. And I'm not just saying that because I'll lose my commission if you go with Minosi. Seven-thousand-five-hundred I can kiss goodbye."

"We'll discuss that later," Nick said. "What intrigues me

is why they picked on you for Maria. Conan met you at my exhibition. Maybe originally he just wanted to get me for the Minosi, but a year later—about the time *Art World* published my Frageau—Maria suddenly calls you again. They know I did the Frageau, Bert. I don't know how they know, but they know. And if you'd fallen for Maria as you were supposed to, they would have gotten the other Frageaus from you. You didn't go along with that, so Conan's trying to put the muscle on you. And it gives him a good excuse to follow you, search your apartment without much chance that you'll report him to the police. In Italy, affairs of the heart are considered outside of the law," he explained to us.

"But if you exhibit the painting at the Minosi, Lingini probably won't see it, and she's the one who's willing to pay big bucks," Bert pointed out. "Mega bucks, Nick. She said whatever Boisvert offered, she'd pay more."

"She'll see it. You're forgetting, Maria was at her party last night," Nick countered. "An . . . interesting connection, that."

After I had considered this interesting fact, I began to have a few doubts. "That doesn't necessarily mean they're working together. They might just be acquaintances, through art dealings."

"The Minosi isn't the kind of place Lingini shops for art," Bert thought. "Not the same league at all."

Undaunted, I said, "Well then, they might actually be competitors for the Frageau, and Lingini just wanted to keep an eye on the competition. If that's how it is, Maria won't call the Contessa."

Nick just smiled unconcernedly. "She'll call. The Contessa has practically said she'll pay anything for a Frageau. The Minosi Gallery wants the painting to sell, not to keep. Why wouldn't they notify the highest bidder?"

"If it was a matter of keeping an eye on the competition, why wasn't Conan at the party?" Bert asked. "He owns the Minosi. Maria's just his helper."

Nick listened, unperturbed. "I'll phone Lingini tomorrow morning to make sure she knows the picture's there. One way or the other, it should be an interesting morning. And now we'll forget about the case. We've been promising to show the ladies around Rome, Bert. The rain's stopped. Let's go out on the town."

Nancy and I exchanged a blissful smile. "You were going to take us to the Sound and Light show at the Forum," I reminded them. "If we hurry, we can catch it."

Bert glanced at his watch. "We better get a hustle on."

"What'll you do with the Frageau while we're out of the house?" Nancy asked Nick.

"Stick it back in the oven," Bert suggested. "I don't mean turn the oven on. Just hide it there."

That's what we did. Then Nancy and I got dressed in our fanciest clothes and went out to see, at last, the Forum, and enjoy a night on the town.

CHAPTER 13

Floodlights shone on statues and columns as we drove down the Corso. The Forum, as they say, needs no introduction. Bert had been there often and acted as our guide. He suggested we approach it from the Campidoglio. Nick parked the car and we had our first view from the deck. A melancholy graveyard air hung over the scene. The stumps of ruined columns looked like headstones, bathed in eerie light. Some longer column shafts and a few arches had escaped the depredations of war and time and man, and reared into the blue-black sky, where a ghostly white moon shone. Behind it all the swell of the Palatine Hill formed a ragged backdrop. The outline of individual trees lent a touch of nature to all the ruined grandeur of old Rome. Umbrella pines hovered protectively amidst the palms, cedars, and of course, the ever-present cypresses that are as much a part of Italy as the wine or language.

"What was the Forum, exactly, before it became a ruin?" Nancy asked.

"It was Rome," Bert said simply. "Law courts, temples, market, prison, theater, villas. That," he pointed to three columns, "is Julius Caesar's Forum. Yessir, they stuck it to poor old Julius, the Ides of March. *Et tu, Brute.*"

"Imagine, and it's still here," Nancy said, in an awed voice.

"It's back," Bert corrected.

"Where did it go?"

"Underground. Buried. This was a cowfield for centuries. Cow cookies all over the greatest show on earth. It was only dug up in the nineteenth century. People used to take the marble for other buildings, but the government watches the place like a hawk now. I think that pedestal in your house is from here, isn't it, Nick?"

"That's the legend. My grandfather gave it to my mother. It's a family heirloom."

As our eyes became accustomed to the eerie lighting, we could pick out a few residual bits of architecture from amongst the featureless brickwork remains. One pretty doorway, leading nowhere, was in good repair. Bert said the columns and acanthus leaves at the top were nearly perfect, but the architrave was crumbling and the pediment was half gone. The ruins were softened by vines and grass and shrubs. Bert quoted half forgotten old historical names, but I was content to just look and absorb the mood of romantic desolation, because I knew I wouldn't recall the details anyway. Some of it sounded like legend, but there really were Vestal Virgins. A part of their temple remained. He spoke of Estruscan kings and various Caesars and Augustuses, on through the Renaissance and right up to Mussolini.

As he explained, the scene came alive. In imagination, walls rose again, lintels spanned the columns and domes appeared above the arches. I could almost hear the tramp of Roman legions, imagine the sun gleaming on armor, and flags waving. Or maybe I was just remembering scenes from *Quo Vadis*. Anyway it was thrilling. It had been here forever, that was what I had difficulty grasping. When I think of old, in terms of architecture, I tend to think of Williamsburg, but Monticello would be a baby here. Rome was ancient. That was why a medieval doorway would suddenly catch my eye in some cobblestoned alley, and throw me for a loop. That was why I occasionally saw a fine marble archway leading into a hovel of a house. The layers of history revealed themselves in this interesting way.

"The orchestra plays in the Basilica of Maxentius," Bert said. "Want to have a listen?"

He led us to the basilica, a ruin of course, but the vaulted roof remained and there was seating in front of it. An orchestra—a large one—was dwarfed in the cavernous space, giving some idea of the monumental size of the original edifice. Gold lights shone from above. They were playing something form *The Barber of Seville*. "Rossini should be sung," Bert humphed. I wondered if he'd heard a tourist say that before, but maybe I'm just revealing my prejudice against him. He had surprised me with his knowledge of the place. Did the soul of a romantic lurk beneath his desperate bravado?

There was a large crowd. In the privacy of darkness, I noticed some men had their arms around women's shoulders. Some of them were necking, but not as passionately as couples did in Paris. Nancy's head leaned away from me, and I saw Bert's arm go around her shoulders, pulling her against him. I waited, wondering if Nick would follow suit. It had been a romantic evening, and I hoped he would. He just reached out and took my hand. We smiled. He looked at the row in front of us, where one couple were becoming quite Parisian. Then he checked the row behind us to see how they were behaving, or maybe to make sure no one there would recognize him, before he became amorous.

I expected to feel his hand withdraw from mine, but not quite so convulsively as it did, lifting my skirt in the process. I expected the arm would then go around my shoulder. I really didn't expect him to jump to his feet and shout, "Holy Christ, it's him!" The audience turned and gave various indications of their disgust. The Italians are quite uninhibited in that respect. Just as well I didn't know what they were saying. Certain polylingual hand signals gave the general idea.

Nick didn't sit down and try to hide his head after this shameful exhibition. He began an ungainly exit. Hemmed in by a full row, he leapt over the back of the seat to the row behind, where he only had to annoy six patrons before he got to the aisle. Bert and Nancy quit smooching long enough to ask what was going on.

"He saw somebody, and took off like a bat out of hell," I said.

"Did you see who it was?" Nancy asked.

"No, but it was a man. He said 'It's him.' Maybe it was Boisvert."

Bert paled visibly. "Or Conan."

A muted hiss of "Shhh" and "*Silenzio*" came at us from front and rear.

"He wouldn't have chased Conan. He would have ducked," I whispered.

"Was it Claude or Réné?" Nancy asked.

"I didn't see who it was."

The "Shhh!" and "*Silenzio*" were no longer muted, and a few less discreet utterances were added to the chorus. We decided this conversation should be resumed beyond the basilica and left in disgrace, receiving a baleful glare from the owner of every knee we had to jar in the process. By the time we got out, there was nothing to see but semi-darkness, and the vast, stretching length of the Forum.

"Maybe we should split up," Bert said.

"What for? I'm not going looking for trouble alone," Nancy declared.

Bert rubbed his chin, probably figuring the chances that it wasn't Conan, and finally loped off. Nancy and I stayed outside the basilica, where we could run back in for safety if anyone with a gun should show up.

"I wonder if Nick brought his gun," I said.

"I heard him tell Bert he was putting it in his car. Maybe he went there to get it."

"We'll wait five minutes. If they don't come back, we'll go to the car."

Nick was back within two minutes. "I lost him," he said.

"Who was it?" Nancy and I demanded in unison.

"Claude. He's following me. He must be. He wouldn't just coincidentally show up here. He was standing at the back of the hall, staring at me." Nancy didn't use the word synchronicity. "Where's Bert?" he asked.

"Looking for you," she said.

In ten or so minutes, Bert came back, and Nick told him about Claude. "What do you figure he's after?" Bert asked.

"I'll be damned if I know."

"The Frageau?" Nancy suggested.

"They've already stolen all the Frageaus except the new one. They can't know I've done another."

"They might, if they're following you. Maybe they peeked in your window," she said.

I said, "Then they'd know it's in the oven."

"*Was* in the oven," Bert added, with a knowing look. "Maybe we'd better check it out."

"If it's the painting they're after, they wouldn't be following me," Nick insisted. "Claude could see at a glance I wasn't carrying a painting."

"You could have it hidden in your car," Bert said.

I thought the incident had set Bert's nerves on edge. He was just afraid Conan might be lurking behind a column, and wanted to get out of the Forum. The romantic atmosphere had long since evaporated. None of us was in the mood for Rossini after the interruption, and we decided to leave.

There were hundreds of cars parked beyond the Forum. Nick took the idea that if we skulked in the shadows, Claude might show up to claim one of them, and he'd beat the truth out of him. We also kept our eyes open for a black Jag.

"There's another parking lot," Bert said. "Not everybody knows about this one. I led you here because I wanted the girls to see the Forum from the deck first. It's the best view. Want I should take a nip over to the other lot, Nick?"

"Sure, why not?"

Bert trotted off alone. Nancy said, "We should have worn sneakers, Lana." She looked down at her ultra-high heeled sandals, that she wore in an effort to diminish her ankles.

Nick went to see if the car had been broken into. I don't know how he could tell. He had locked it, but the front door on the passenger's side was already so mangled that a mere crowbar to the door would hardly be noticeable. He didn't think anyone had been working on it. We stood around for another ten minutes, scanning everyone who came or left the lot, then Bert came back.

"Zilch. Zippo," he said. "Anything happen here?"

"No. We might as well leave," Nick told him.

We all piled in. Nick put the key in the ignition, turned it. Nothing happened. He kept turning it harder and ramming his foot on the gas, but there wasn't even a sniffle from the engine, much less a cough or wheeze. "I hate the infernal combustion engine!" he growled.

"It requires gas, my friend," Bert told him. "Have you let it run dry again?" The bored way he said it indicated this was a fairly frequent occurence.

"The gauge only fell to empty this afternoon. I can usually run a day or two on empty."

I heard Nancy in the backseat mutter, "The man needs a keeper."

Although I was annoyed with her, I tended to agree. There is no excuse for a man's running out of gas unless he's on a back road with his girlfriend.

"I'll have a look under the hood," Bert said, and I got out to let him out.

Nick, with apparently zero knowledge of cars, got out and checked all the tires for flatness. When they proved innocent, he kicked them for good measure. We all stood around, knowing in our bones the tank was empty. And even if it wasn't, I didn't have much faith that Bert could resuscitate the engine. He reached into the darkness, took out a little box of wax matches (from the Risorgimento) and lit one. Nancy held it for him, and kept lighting more matches as he examined the rat's nest of belts and fans and things, muttering, "That seems all right," as he worked. He pulled at a nest of wires, jiggled the metal dome they were attached to like an octopus and said, "Ah ha! Just as I suspected! He's been at this distributor cap. It's loose. If he took the rotor, we're S.O.L." He unscrewed the dome with all the wires sticking out of tubes on top and said, "Yup, it's gone. He took out the rotor. We might as well call a garage."

"What does it look like?" I asked.

"It's a little black cylinder, pointed on one end, that goes on here," he said, pointing to a small shaft. "He wouldn't have left it lying around. He took it out so we couldn't leave."

I think it is perhaps impossible for a man to keep his head out of a car with the hood up. Nick was there, probing around. "He must have been in a hurry if he left the cap loose. Maybe he just tossed it in here." He began feeling around.

"You have to open the car to get under the hood. Someone *did* break in," I said. Nick grunted assent.

Nancy held matches while they searched, and I stood back to be out of the way. I looked idly around the ground, not thinking it very likely I'd find the rotor. It struck me as strange, by which I mean suspicious, that Bert had found the trouble so quickly. Was this one of the things all men knew and women didn't? Was it like keeping score in football and hockey, and steering with the palm of the hand? Or did Bert know because he had advance knowledge? Maybe he had done it himself, when he ran off from the basilica to look for Nick and Claude. He'd been gone quite a while.

And if so, why had he done it? In case we spotted someone and wanted to follow him/her? Was he working with Boisvert? Or perhaps with Claude, or the Contessa whom he had been so eager to phone? Or the whole gang of them? I stepped back as a couple of women came toward their car, and felt something crunch under my foot. I looked down and saw a little black thing, not much bigger than my thumb. I picked it up; it was a cylinder with some metal on one end.

"Is this what you're looking for?" I called.

Nick came running. "She found it!" he laughed. "The guy must have just tossed it over his shoulder. Good work, Lana!"

Bert put the rotor back in and restored the distributor cap. The car, despite the gas gauge that registered empty, started up on the first try. "Where are we going?" Nancy asked.

"Home first, to check up on my Frageau," Nick replied.

"Don't you think we should cruise around a bit and see if we can pick up Claude's trail?" Bert suggested.

That too sounded suspicious. If Bert had disabled the car, intending to delay us, he must be chewing nails that I had found the rotor. Why hadn't he gotten rid of it more permanently? "Let's go right home," I said.

"He must be around here some place," Bert insisted. "Let's tour around the Campidoglio."

"Since someone put Nick's car out of commission, he obviously wants to keep Nick away from his house. I think we should go there immediately," I said.

"Maybe whoever did it just wanted to stop Nick from following him, in case he was seen," Bert countered.

After a little more discussion, we all got into the car and Nick headed straight to his place. I kept thinking how Bert had tried to delay our going there. Though actually he was the one who first suggested we go back and check the oven. I wanted to like Bert and trust him, but at every turn, he seemed to act suspiciously. And if he was involved in some dirty deal behind Nick's back after Nick treated him so generously, I didn't intend to let him get away with it.

CHAPTER 14

We rushed in and all ran directly to the kitchen. The Frageau was there in the oven, undamaged. We felt we had earned a drink, and opted for a corked bottle of wine, in case someone had been slipping a mickey into an opened bottle. We sat around the glass-topped coffee table.

"I wonder why Claude was following me," Nick said.

"Maybe he was planning to shoot you," I suggested.

Nick gave a lazy smile and said, "Wishful thinking."

Bert shook his head. "At least he'd didn't take a potshot at you. Of course that may have been the intention. Maybe that's why he rigged your car, so you'd be standing around—easy to pick you off."

A shiver of fear ran up my spine. This rather slick suggestion detoured any taint of suspicion from Bert, and annoyed me. "We don't know that Claude rigged the car. For that matter, it wasn't Claude who shot at Nick. It was Boisvert's friend."

"Boisvert obviously brought more than one friend," Bert said. "It's as plain as the nose on your face. Where we ran into Claude was at the Risorgimento, where you girls saw Boisvert. He flipped when you told him you were Frageau, Lana. He lied to Nick, and he's French. What do you want, a sworn statement?"

"He's right," Nick said, frowning.

"If his intention was to shoot you, why didn't he do it?"

I asked. "You were standing around the car, right out in the open. He could have got you."

"Maybe he couldn't get a clean shot," Bert suggested. "You should get yourself a bullet-proof vest, Nick. And wear a helmet."

"Comforting thought!" Nick got up and closed the drapes. "He might be out there now. He must lurk nearby, or how did he know we were going to the Forum?" A tingle of fear ran around the room as we sipped at the wine for courage.

"How did you know what was wrong with the car, Bert?" I asked.

"That's the oldest trick in the book. We used to do it to old Gouty Buckland's car at high school. Every Friday afternoon the poor guy couldn't get his car started. It took him a month to catch on. He was convinced rotors wore out in a week—vanished. He started carrying a spare in his glove compartment. What a dope."

I did remember the joke of Mr. Buckland's car always failing him after school on Friday. The kids used to stand around the street, watching him try to get it going. It explained Bert's lighting on the rotor tonight. But it didn't account for his reluctance to come right home. Maybe our early arrival was all that prevented Claude from breaking in and stealing the Frageau.

It was still not very late, and there was some talk of our continuing our night on the town. "We made it home in one piece. Let's stay put," I suggested.

"We've talked ourselves into a state of siege," Nick objected. "Nobody's trying to kill me. We promised you a night out. We're going to deliver."

"First you'd better put the Frageau in some safe place," I said aside to Nick, while Bert was busy with Nancy.

"I'll hide it in the wine cellar," he said, and took it out of the room. I noticed Bert watched him, but he couldn't see which way he went.

"Where's Nick taking the picture?" he asked.

"He's going to put it under his bed," I said blandly, "in case Claude has designs on it."

Nick came back and I hastily turned the conversation away from where Nick had hidden the picture. "So, where shall we go?" I asked brightly.

We talked about that while we went to the car. Bert said he was hungry, and kept mentioning different restaurants. Nancy and I wanted to go downtown and walk first, to see Rome by night, maybe do the Italian equivalent of pub crawling. I wondered if Bert's hunger was designed to give him access to a phone. Just as we were getting into the car, he said, "Just hold on a minute, will you? I have to answer nature's call." He ran back to the house, and I stayed out of the car, watching the windows to see where lights went on. I noticed he had his own key to Nick's house. Nick kept the doors locked, especially at this time.

The light in the front hallway went on. None upstairs— but then I didn't think he planned to move the painting. He was just using the phone to let his friends know the house would be empty. I strolled down past the driveway to get a view of the studio, that faced the left side. If he used the phone, he did it by touch. The lights didn't go on. Bert reappeared in about the length of time it would take to go to the washroom—or make a phone call. He had those matches from the Risorgimento.

Nick turned left off the main road before we reached the Corso. I didn't know my way around Rome very well, but I knew he wasn't heading right downtown, and asked where he was going.

"Just curious," he said. "I'm going to drive past the Contessa's place, and see if she has company."

"Do you mean Boisvert, or Claude, or who?"

"Boisvert, or the man who shot at me, or Claude, or even Maria. She was at the party. I don't know who. We probably won't see anything at all, but I'm just curious to learn what Rosa's involvement in all this is. I wonder if she got in touch with Boisvert this morning."

"You won't get very close with those dogs patrolling the grounds."

"You don't have to get very close to watch."

"With your eyes you'd have to have your nose glued to the window."

"You're going the wrong way, Nick," Bert called. He hadn't overheard our private conversation.

"Just a slight detour."

"Where to?"

"Contessa Lingini's, to see if any of our 'friends' are there," Nick said.

"Don't forget you're running low on gas. Why don't you try to find a station?"

With a phone, so he could alert the Contessa? Every word Bert uttered, every move he made came under scrutiny. More often than not I found something suspicious, but never enough to air my suspicions in front of his friends. Nancy would only get angry, and Nick trusted his old buddy. And I'd been wrong about Bert before. Nick paid no attention to the idea of an empty gas tank requiring gas. He drove to the Pincian Hill and parked in the shadows with a view of the villa across the street, not close enough that we'd be spotted. There were plenty of lights on, but we didn't intend to go window peeking. We just sat and looked. Her Bentley wasn't in view. There was a small, dark red car in the driveway, not the Jag that Boisvert's drove when he shot at Nick.

Bert leaned his head over the seat and said, "It seems she has company."

"Possibly," Nick agreed. "Or that could be the Conte's car, or more likely a friend's—maybe even a car she provides for the servants. I'm going to check out the license plate so we'll recognize it if we see it again. You get in the driver's seat, Bert, in case we want to take off in a hurry." He got out and scuttled closer to the villa, straining his eyes. He wasn't wearing his glasses, so I joined him. "Can you make anything out?" he asked.

"The big numbers on the back say R something LO on top, 2439 on the bottom. There's one of those stickers with the wolf suckling Romulus and Remus." These were very common in Rome. Nancy had bought one to take home for her Escort.

"Do you think we should risk crossing the street and trying for the windows?"

My answer was an unequivocal, "No."

"You go back to the car."

"Nick, you won't be able to see anything anyway."

"Let me borrow your glasses. You're short-sighted, too." He actually reached out his hand for my glasses.

"I have an astigmatism. Nancy's right. You *do* need a keeper." There was a childlike simplicity to Nick that could always surprise me, and touch off a hitherto buried maternal instinct. Perhaps it was the artistic streak that kept him free of reality. Such things as cars needing gas, individual prescriptions for people's spectacles, and the destructive power of pit bull terriers didn't occur to him.

I took his hand. "You're going back to the car."

He cocked his head to one side to think about it. We were in this pose, me yanking at his arm, Nick contemplating, when the front door of the villa opened. Nick, the ass, came to attention and made a motion of going closer to see who it was, and possibly getting his head blown off in the process. I held him back and we both watched as the man on the doorstep looked up and down the street. Within a second, he'd be looking across the road. I put my arms around Nick's neck and pulled his head down to mine. Lovers, like children, are free of suspicion, and unlike children, are not at all an uncommon sight in the shadows of Rome at night.

When I had his head safely averted and his physique disguised by hunching over me, I whispered, "Now we can look. Who is it?"

A dark glitter of eyes, a smiling flash of white teeth, and an increased pressure of his arms told me Nick had forgotten the man. "Who cares?" he asked softly, and kissed me. For a breathless moment, I forgot the man, too. It's the unexpected embraces that thrill. The air of danger added something to the experience of being thoroughly embraced by an accomplished Adonis. He crushed me against his chest with a mannish vigor. One hand rose to fondle the nape of my neck, and firm my head for the attack.

"I knew you couldn't be all ice," he murmured in my ear.

That compliment cooled my ardor somewhat, and brought me back to reality. With a frosty gaze I said, "Well, do you recognize him?"

Nick squinted across the street. I looked, and had no difficulty recognizing Claude. He was still in the white shirt he'd worn at the restaurant. The Contessa called to him softly from the doorway in her lovely French, but with an air of exasperation. "Don't do anything else till you hear from me. You'll spoil all my plans."

"*C'est mon affaire aussi,*" he called back, rather angrily. It's my business, too.

"It's Claude," I told Nick.

"I'm not deaf, just blind. I recognized his voice. He was reporting to her that he'd spotted me—and probably rigged my car. We'll follow him."

We waited till Claude got in his car and pulled out, so that he wouldn't recognize us. He turned left, and we hurried toward the Alfa-Romeo. Just as we approached it, Bert coasted alongside us. Nick's car, unfortunately, was pointed the other way. I couldn't blame that on Bert. In fact, it seemed he was really trying to be helpful. I clambered in the backseat with Nancy, Nick got in front with Bert at the wheel, but by the time they got turned around, Claude had disappeared down some side street. We drove around for a while, looking for him, but without success. We told Bert and Nancy what we had heard as we drove.

"We've lost him. Like looking for a nickel in a haystack," Bert said. I noted the Freudian slip. He had an obsession with money. "Shall we go to a bar?"

"Maybe we should go back to Nick's place," I said. "Because of the painting."

"Yeah, under your bed's the first place they'll look for it," Bert warned Nick.

"It isn't under my bed. I hid it in the wine cellar."

Bert didn't turn around, but I could feel his eyes narrowing. His voice was just a little thin when he said, "I must have misunderstood. I thought Lana said you were hiding it under your bed."

So he now knew that I still harbored a few suspicions of him. I didn't bother inventing any misunderstanding, with naive Nick there to contradict me. There was no point. I just felt lousy instead. We drove home and had another glass of wine and some bread and cheese. Bert and I sat across from each other, both letting on nothing had happened. Nick checked the cellar and reported that the Frageau was safe. He left it there for safekeeping through the night.

"What do you think the Contessa meant by telling Claude not to do anything else?" Nancy asked. "Do you think she was referring to his tailing you to the Forum, Nick?"

"Probably. I don't know what else he's been up to. More interesting is his complaint that it's his business, *too*. That doesn't sound as though they're working together, exactly. More like one of them horned in, don't you think?"

"It sounds as if Claude is the horner-inner," Bert said. "He said 'too.' It was his business, *too*—that kind of implies it's mostly Lingini's business, doesn't it?"

"Then Lingini must be working with Boisvert," I deduced. "I don't see how else she got involved. How could they have met up, him in Paris, her in Rome?"

We puzzled over it for a while. "Boisvert must have co-opted her," Nick thought aloud. "She's obviously no stranger to France. She speaks beautiful French. He probably met her at some gallery in Paris. I wouldn't have thought he ran with her elite pack—he didn't in the old days. If her reputation has picked up an aroma since then, he might have learned about it and approached her."

"It's funny Boisvert is keeping such a low profile," Bert said. "Alberto thinks he spotted him at the Quattrocento, but we're not even sure it was him. None of us have actually *seen* him, except Nancy. She thinks she saw him at the Risorgimento, but we couldn't find him. Maybe it was just some guy with a big nose. Maybe he's not even here, in Rome."

"Of course he's here," Nancy exclaimed. "I recognized him from the picture. It was certainly him. All the other suspects turned up at the Risorgimento. It wasn't just coincidence that Claude was there, and Lingini came in, looking for a light."

"He's here, engineering the whole thing," Nick said. "He's just being careful to keep out of my way. And of course he's arranging an airtight alibi for himself, in case any of his friends succeed in killing me. He knows it would come out eventually that I'm Frageau, now that my *Rouge et Noir* study has been in *Art World*. He'd have some explaining to do. You can bet he'll be in some public place, surrounded by people that can identify him, when I'm shot."

"I told you we shouldn't have gone back out!" I complained. "You're a sitting duck, Nick. You should get out of town."

"I won't be run out of my own home. Not by that fool of a Boisvert, or Réné or Claude."

"Who *is* Claude?" I pondered. "If he's horning in on Boisvert and Lingini, how did he find out anything about Frageau? Could he be working for Fargé, Edouard's father?"

"He could *be* Fargé, for all we know," Bert said. "Maybe he followed Boisvert to Rome, trying to learn what he's up to. He hasn't really done anything except follow Nick. He might have followed you to the Risorgimento. That's where you first spotted him. Maybe he's just trying to find out if Boisvert fed him a load of crap."

"He already seemed to know that. But how can we account for his knowing the Contessa?" Nick said.

"He followed you—or Boisvert—to her. Maybe he told her about Boisvert claiming his son's body. That'd account for him saying it was his business, too."

"If he's getting in Boisvert's way, I'm not the only one that should wear a bullet-proof vest," Nick said. "I should warn him that Boisvert plays for keeps."

"Next time you spot him following you, you want to tell him that," Nancy said sarcastically. "He's not Fargé. He's working with Boisvert. If he had nothing to hide, he'd talk to you, instead of running like a hare every time you spot him."

The wine sank lower in the bottle as we discussed possibilities. Nick opened another bottle, and before we all got so tight we forgot who slept where, I suggested we go to bed.

"Like a good little icicle," Nick said, with a mocking grin. "You don't want to drink too much alcohol. It prevents freezing."

"And destroys the brain cells. That's probably what happened to yours."

"Probably, but it's left the rest of my body intact," he said, and on that suggestive note, he left.

When Nancy came upstairs about a quarter of an hour later, I let on I was asleep, because I thought Bert had probably told her about my saying the painting was under Nick's bed. She'd know I had lied, and would soon figure out why. I didn't feel like an argument at that late hour, and she and Bert were becoming so lovey-dovey she'd certainly take me to task. I couldn't make up my mind about Bert. Sometimes he seemed all right. The old saying, "As the twig bends, so grows the tree," kept running through my mind. And Bert had been a little crooked as a twig.

CHAPTER 15

This story is enough to give school teachers a bad reputation. Neither I nor Nancy usually drink so much, but it was our vacation, and in the morning I had another fuzzy head. Above the niggling pain in my temple wafted memories of the Forum by moonlight, with the crumbling grandeur of old Rome spreading under the soft, velvet, star-spangled sky. Then I remembered the less romantic events that followed. I was happy to see that Nancy was already up and out of the room, even if she had left her nighttime brassiere on the dresser, and the bathroom would be a shambles. I took her nightie off the shower rod, folded up her towels and turned on the water.

A shower helped to dissipate the grogginess. Nothing had been said of discontinuing the plan of offering the Frageau to the Minosi Gallery, so I assumed it was still on. It seemed risky to me, but Nick was determined to prove he was macho and capable. Anticipation added haste to my dressing, although it was only eight o'clock, and obviously too early to call the gallery or the Contessa. Lingini probably slept till noon.

The first glimpse of Nick at the table put a reluctant smile on my lips. He had been staring at the doorway, waiting for me. His spontaneous smile greeted me when I entered, and his eyes glowed a warm welcome. Nancy and Bert were there, too, all of us looking tired and wan. Coffee restored the color to our cheeks and a couple of croissants and four thin slices of melon filled our empty stomachs, or at least allayed the ache.

I thought Nancy must have apologized to Bert for me, or explained away my insinuating question. There was a mood of conviviality that couldn't be explained otherwise. At such moments, it was hard to go on mistrusting Bert. What I mentally called "evidence" was all circumstantial.

"Isn't this great?" Bert said two or three times. "Gee, it's nice being with Americans again. You understand everything I say, and vice versa. I'm going to miss you guys," he said, but it was mostly Nancy he gazed at, with a quiver of his lips.

"The planes fly both ways, Bert," she said. "Don't you ever plan to come home?"

"Home?" he asked, with a world-weary look. "What is there for someone like me in Troy?"

I took it for a rhetorical question, meaning he was too cosmopolitan to be amused at our provinciality. Nancy understood him better. She took him seriously, and answered, "We have lots of industries now. I bet you could get a good job as a salesman, or in marketing or P.R. or something."

"The old man left me the house," he said, consideringly.

Nancy looked her encouragement. "It'd be wonderful to have you back there."

"Are my tenants wrecking the place?"

"No, actually it looks bet— it looks fine. They planted peonies in the backyard—there in the corner where your dad used to pile—uh—refuse," she said vaguely. Mrs. Garr referred to the heap of discarded furniture that marred their yard as compost. The indignant neighbors had called a cast-off stuffed chair and a broken stove garbage.

He stared into the fruit bowl with a faraway look in his eyes. "Peonies in the backyard. That sure sounds homey. They're the little skinny yellow flowers that shoot up early in spring?"

"No, they're the big bushy ones that come in early summer. They're pink and white and red. If you put siding over the clapboard of your house, Bert, or cedar shingles, it'd look just fine," Nancy added. A hopeful question lit her green eyes. I knew what she had in her mind—how cozy it would be, living just two houses down from her mother. Bert looked at her. You could almost feel the air tremble with a proposal. She blushed. I looked at Nick.

"It's going to be another warm day," he said. "Just look at that sun." It streamed through the window, and cast dancing shadows on the floor. Those who are acclimatized to the sizzling inferno of Rome in July call it warm. I looked forward to another scorcher. "Shall we take our coffee out to the terrace?"

"You go ahead," Bert said. His eyes never left Nancy's.

We took our cups outside to let them have privacy. We went to the balustrade and looked over the rooftops and spires. The greenery shone after its rain bath. "I'll miss Bert," Nick said wistfully.

"You think he's going to propose?"

"He probably has, by now. He could be my agent for the States. New York isn't that far from Troy. The Contessa was wondering why I don't exhibit in New York. Maybe it's time for it."

I didn't say anything. This didn't seem the right moment to hint that Bert had been missing for ten minutes last night, and might have met up with Claude, or put Nick's car out of commission himself. Nick knew him better than I did, and if he trusted Bert, I wasn't going to put my foot in it again.

Quite aside from any criminal behavior, however, Bert Garr didn't strike me as the optimum agent, but what did I know? He'd done all right by Nick so far. Really my mind was more attuned to the fact that Nick had no intention of returning to the States himself. His home was here. His tempera works were imbued with the soul of Italy. Why would he want to leave this lovely villa and go to Troy, where half the year it was so cold you could hardly stick your nose out the door? A famous artist in Troy would be like a bird in the sea, or a fish in the sky. It would be the wrong ambience.

"I couldn't hack the winters myself," he said, almost as though he'd been reading my mind.

My throat felt tight. "They're pretty grim all right."

"Why do you stay on there?"

"I'm used to it. I like the change of seasons. Spring and fall are beautiful," I said, on the defense. "Rome's much too hot in the summer to suit me."

"It's warm, but the winters are so long and cold in New York." He gave an involuntary shudder at the memory.

It was hard to believe snow really existed, out on the terrace with the sun streaming down. The sky was an incredible azure blue, with puffs of cotton wool clouds hanging motionless above. Nick took my hand and smiled. I felt like crying. I smiled back. "Too long," he said. "I could never spend winter in New York. My soul would freeze. It was those winters that my mother couldn't take. I have something of her Latin streak in me."

"That figures." It's strange what mundane conversations people have at moments of high anxiety. We so often revert to nonverbal communication. I just looked at him, waiting, wondering if he'd make any mention, however tenuous, regarding my feelings for a winter in Rome.

He drank his coffee distractedly, and soon said, "Shouldn't you phone your group in Salerno and let them know where you are?"

"What I should tell them is when we'll be rejoining them."

"You and Nancy will want to discuss it."

We went back in a little later. Bert was sitting with his arm over Nancy's shoulder, but they didn't make any announcement. Nick went to wrap up the Frageau, I cleared the table and stacked the dishwasher, and Bert and Nancy went out to the terrace. I went to the studio to phone Salerno. Ron was out with the group. I left a message and said we'd phone again that evening. Then I went back to the kitchen to say goodbye. As I lovingly wiped the tiled counter and put things away, I wondered what message I'd be giving Ron Evereton.

Lana Morton would be rejoining the tour, but Nancy Bankes wouldn't? No, the tour was paid for. Nancy would probably finish it and let Bert wind up his business in

Rome. Whatever happened during the remaining weeks of our European visit, it wouldn't hold a candle to these few days. I watered the herbs on the windowsill, breathing in the pungent air of oregano and parsley and marjoram. When we got back to Troy, Nancy would be preparing for her wedding. It would be a very large, white extravaganza. Nancy had been waiting for a wedding since she was about six years old. She had a hope chest and a clothes closet full of china and linen. I had a martini pitcher and six glasses bought at a sale, and I didn't even like martinis. Maybe Nick would come for the wedding . . .

At ten o'clock, Nick phoned the Minosi Gallery. He had decided to say he was no longer Bert's client, as a pretext for calling them. We all stood around, listening. "Signorina Bambolini?"

"Is that Maria's name?" Nancy whispered, and laughed.

Nick spoke in Italian, identifying himself and asking if the Minosi would be interested in exhibiting him. Bert translated roughly for us, but it was hardly necessary. We could hear the excited eagerness in Maria's voice. *"Meravigliosa." "Incantevole."* Nick hung up the phone and smiled. "I'm to take the painting down right away. I didn't tell her it's from my French Frustration period. It should be interesting to see her reaction."

"You were going to phone Lingini," Bert reminded him. "Is that still on after last night?"

"More than ever." He dialed again. *"Pronto, la Contessa, per piacere."* A pause. *"Rosa? Questò è Niccolò."*

"Ah, Niccolò!" Her voice held the same eager excitement as Maria's. Soon he replaced the receiver and gave another of his Machiavellian smiles.

"What did she say?" we demanded, more or less in unison.

"She was very interested. She asked me why the Minosi?"

"It's a logical question, isn't it?" I asked.

"Oh, very, but I hadn't told her what gallery the painting would be at. I just told her it wasn't being exhibited at the Quattrocento. As the style was so different, I had decided to put it with a gallery. Just before she hung up, she said, 'I'll go down to the Minosi this morning.' But I purposely didn't give her the name. She knew which gallery."

"Maria must have phoned her," Bert suggested.

Nick looked doubtful. "She didn't have time. There were hardly thirty seconds between calls. How did Rosa know? They're all working together: Boisvert, Claude, Maria, Lingini."

"Maria knows Lingini wants the picture, and is willing to pay top dollar for it," Nancy countered. "Maybe she phoned the Contessa the instant you hung up."

Before Nick left, we held a short conference. "Just what exactly is supposed to happen next?" I demanded. "I mean you talked about a catalyst, Nick, but do you really have any idea just what effect this catalyst might have? Some catalysts cause explosions."

"And some cause various particles to fuse," he added. "I seem to be that sort. One characteristic of a catalyst is that the catalytic agent itself is not permanently changed."

"You're not a chemical. Boisvert's friend had a gun, remember."

"So do I. Anyway, they'd never shoot me at the gallery. If they're all in it together, they don't want my death tied to the gallery. If they're in competition, they wouldn't shoot me with witnesses present."

"If they're in cahoots, what's to prevent them from killing you and moving your body from the gallery?"

He gave a lazy smile. "You sound as if you care, Lana."

I cared so much my insides were shaking. Nick continued, "I want to see who else comes running to the Minosi Gallery. Will Boisvert, for instance, come trotting? How else did Conan know I'm Fragéau, except through Boisvert? He's the only one who knew."

"I wish the Interpol agent, who probably doesn't even exist, would come trotting," I said. "This could get very dangerous."

"I think of it every time I look at my car windows. I'm taking my gun."

"Be careful, old buddy," Bert cautioned.

"Aren't you going with him?" I asked in alarm. I had always assumed that Bert would go with him. That was part of my fear, yet now that he wasn't going, it seemed even worse. I didn't want Nick to go alone into that den of thieves.

"How can I? Nick's no longer my client. It'd look odd, to say the least. I can hang around outside if you like, Nick." Bert looked at his watch.

"No, you have your job. No point messing it up," Nick said.

"I've got to be on duty at the Risorgimento at eleven. It doesn't leave me much time."

"You mean you're going back there? To wait tables?" I asked.

He gave a disparaging snort. "I'll be behind the desk within weeks. You can't expect to start at the top."

Was there no engagement then? Nancy looked aggressively disinterested. "You can't let Nick go alone!" I insisted. "It's too dangerous." For some reason, the word alibi darted into my head. I had an intuition, founded on nothing but fear, that Bert knew trouble was going to erupt, and was forging himself an alibi at the hotel.

"You want I should tag along, Nick?" he asked readily. "Just say the word. If you make it real fast, I could squeeze it in." I didn't know what to think of this offer.

"It might be a good idea for somebody to wait outside—just in case I don't come out," Nick said.

My heart clenched. "I'll go." If it was only waiting outside, I could handle that. Bert was too unreliable as a backup anyway.

"Me, too," Nancy offered.

Bert stayed behind to put on his disguise for work; Nancy and I went to the gallery with Nick in the car. While we were getting ready in the washroom she said, "If you're still thinking Bert has anything to do with all this, forget it."

"You don't know any more about it than I do. You only know what he told you, and if he's involved, he wouldn't tell the truth."

"It just so happens he idolizes Nick. Why do you think he

isn't marrying me? He won't leave him. He asked me to stay," she added.

"If you love him, why don't you stay?"

"If he loves me, why won't he come home? I should mean more to him than Nick. We're not Italians, for God's sake. I'd never be happy here."

Nick came out and the three of us got in the car. It coughed and sputtered along, nearly stopping a few times. The jets of wind whistling through the bullet holes were a constant reminder of the sort of company Nick was throwing himself into. He parked across the street a few shops up from the gallery, legally, if he didn't stay longer than half an hour. The Minosi was on a small, artistic thoroughfare, nestled between an antique shop and a jewelry store. It had a mauve door, which made it easy to spot.

Nick said, "You girls stay here. I'll be back soon." I didn't take issue with his use of the juvenile noun. I felt as helpless as a child. He got out and crossed the street. My heart sank to my feet when he went inside carrying the wrapped painting and the mauve door closed behind him.

Nancy, seeing my condition, said, "There's a traffic cop two blocks down. I'll run and get him if trouble breaks out."

"I'm going to peek in the window," I said. Nancy came with me. We approached the gallery like a couple of thieves, wearing our sunglasses as a disguise.

The gallery was small, but fairly respectable as far as architecture and decor went. The paintings in the window were nothing special. One was an inferior pre-Raphaelite nymph cavorting in a meadow, the other a scene of Tuscany that was either very old or wore half a dozen coats of varnish. There were a few people I didn't recognize inside—American tourists to judge by the Reeboks and sun hats. Their presence allayed my fears.

Nancy and I strolled along to the jewelry store, where she became entranced by a tray of engagement rings. I was more interested in the mauve door. After sixty seconds, which seemed like at least half an hour, Nick hadn't come out. I had only seen Maria once, at the Contessa's party, and she hadn't paid much attention to me. "I'm going into the gallery," I said.

"Better let me do it. She might recognize you."

"She saw you, too."

"I'll cover my hair with a kerchief."

We argued for a minute, but in the end, it was Nancy who went in, her identifying mane covered by a kerchief and her face disguised by sunglasses. She just made a quick tour, and came about again. "There's nobody in the shop except Maria and the tourists and Nick. She's trying to get rid of the tourists fast. I noticed she kept looking at Nick with her bedroom eyes. He's safe from anything except possible seduction. The Americans—they're from Minnesota—gave three hundred and fifty dollars in travelers' checks for a picture of the Ponte Vecchio that I wouldn't hang in the basement. Maria couldn't guarantee absolutely it was a Canaletto, but definitely of that period. Both appeared pleased with the transaction. Some poor housewife in Minnesota will have her living room disfigured with that awful brown square."

I wasn't really interested in Maria's sales. "You're sure there's nobody else in the back of the gallery?"

"I don't have X-ray eyes."

"She's just waiting till the tourists leave, then they'll jump him. We better call that cop."

No sooner were the words out of my mouth than the tourists came out, hugging their painting and smiling. I felt as if ten teenagers were breakdancing inside me. When Maria came to the window and closed the blinds, I felt actually nauseous with fear. Then she came to the door, opened it, and looked up and down the street, and closed it again, obviously locking it. We heard the metallic clank of metal on metal. We had left it too late. We couldn't get in now without breaking the door down.

I was in no condition to monitor what was going on in the street. It was Nancy who spotted Conan, and poked me in the ribs. He had never looked more frightening, although he was dressed respectably in a business suit and tie. The man was a mountain of muscle, with the sort of build seen in Mr.

Universe contests, meaty bulges oiled to display the grossly deformed human body. The suit only emphasized his inhuman face and jerky, muscle-bound stride. I thought of Bert's mottled body after Conan had caught him. Nick was willowy. He'd crumple like a reed under those ham-hock fists.

If Conan went in that door, I would definitely have a heart attack. And where else could he possibly be going? Maria had phoned him the minute Nick called, and he had come running. Incredibly, he walked right past, but he looked with interest at the closed blinds, smiled menacingly, and hastened his steps. He turned right at the corner and disappeared.

"I bet he's going in the back way!" I exclaimed.

"We've got to stop him!" Nancy said. She was white with apprehension. "The policeman—oh, he's too far away. They could *kill* him before we get back. But we can't go in empty-handed. We've got to find a weapon."

We ran after Conan, watching which way he went. He turned in at the back of the shop on the corner. We followed at a discreet distance. There was an alleyway. When he stopped a few doors along, we jumped out of sight behind a protruding shack at the rear of one of the shops. We heard the click of a door being unlocked, the faint squawk of an unoiled hinge. When we looked out, he had disappeared.

"He wouldn't be sneaking in the back way if he weren't up to something," I whispered. My throat ached.

"What can we use as a weapon?" Nancy asked.

There were bits of debris littering the lane. Nancy picked up a fallen branch. I wrestled a rusty piece of pipe from the reluctant earth, where it had been planted decades before to hold a wire fence, which was still attached to another pipe some yards along. We crept to the doorway. Conan had left the door ajar in his haste, or perhaps to obviate the possibility of more squawking hinges alerting Nick to his presence. The room appeared to be a storage area. There were two rough tables littered with junk and canvases piled against the wall.

There was a door and a dark hallway at the far side of the

room. After our eyes became accustomed to the gloom we could make out dim shapes. The light bulk at the end of the hallway, hiding and listening, was Conan. Fortunately he was turned sideways, not looking behind him. We ducked out of view and stood listening. The pounding of a pulse in my ears drowned out more useful sounds. I risked a peek. Conan was just taking a shiny revolver from his pocket. With his other hand, he seemed to be doing something to the tip of the muzzle. I thought he was putting a silencer on the gun.

CHAPTER 16

I got a tight grip on my pipe. I stood irresolute, on the verge of going after him. Then he slid the gun into his coat pocket, and I ducked in case he looked around. When I looked again a few seconds later, he was gone. He had gone into the front of the gallery then, where Maria and Nick were discussing the Frageau. Gone with the shiny gun hidden in his pocket. Nick thought they wouldn't kill him there, but what was to prevent them from moving his body? Another corpse would roll up on the banks of the Tiber, as they had been doing from time immemorial. I shouldn't have let him come. He'd only done it to impress me.

We tiptoed into the storeroom and eased our way to the front of the corridor. A curtain separated it from the shop, but a partial view was visible from the edge of the curtain. Maria had already introduced Nick and Conan. They were shaking hands. I noticed the front right pocket of both men's jackets sagged a little, and wondered if Nick had noticed that Conan was armed. Blind as a bat and nervous, he wouldn't notice, but Conan was slyer. He was used to this kind of murderous activity. They began examining the painting. Most of their conversation, in Italian of course, went over my head, but I knew they were surprised that it was an abstract. I could interpret "*meravigliosa*," "*splendente*," and a few other compliments. Then Maria's eyes lowered to the signature and she gasped, "Frageau!" She and Conan exchanged a quick, alarmed, questioning look.

Nick couldn't have failed to notice that. He talked on unconcernedly. I understood some words—Paris, Hansen, *morte*, Frageau, Roma, *cinquanta mille*, and figured that he was saying something like, "This is from my Parisian period. I wouldn't want it confused with a Hansen. There's a bizzare rumor around that I'm dead—as you can see, I'm alive and well, and living in Rome. It's not quite as valuable as a Hansen. Frageau usually sells for approximately fifty thousand, I believe."

"Frageau? But who is that?" Maria asked.

"As guilty as a schoolgirl caught with her knickers down" was the way Nancy described her look later. It was that kind of a look—guilt tinged with uncertainty and fear. Maria looked at Conan, who was fingering his right pocket. Maybe Nick did notice. He began to do the same, while making departure sounds. I prayed like I haven't prayed since I had my tonsils out, and was convinced I was going to die. They'd let him go, and Nancy and I could slip quietly out the back door. It seemed my prayer was going to be answered. Nick turned toward the locked front door, leaving the painting with Maria.

No one followed him. He jiggled the handle; it didn't open. Conan nodded to Maria. She went forward to help him. My jangling nerves began to subside. Maria's hands were on the lock, as though it was jammed or something. Nick reached forward to help her, with his back to Conan. That was when Conan made his move. His massive, ungainly frame glided forward as agiley as a cat, while his right hand drew the gun from his pocket. I underestimated Nick. With equal speed and agility, he got Maria's body wedged between his and Nick's gun. In his hand, he, too, held a pistol.

It was a standoff. Nick barked a few words at Conan. Conan looked at his gun, Maria hollered something obscene-sounding at Conan, and he tossed the gun to the floor. But Nick still wasn't out of the shop, and he was out-numbered. Nancy and I exchanged a scared stiff look and rushed forward. There were some excited exclamations from Maria and Conan. Nancy beat me to Conan's gun by inches. I unlocked the front door and we all scampered out into the street. Escape was foremost in our minds. Any calling of police would be done with walls and doors between us and Conan. Even without a gun, he could inflict serious damage. We did some speed-walking away from the gallery, without paying much attention to where we were going. I clung on to Nick's hand as if an avenging angel might sweep out of the sky and take him away from me. Nick was equally tenacious.

"Did you spot Conan, or why did you decide to come to my rescue?" Nick asked. Perspiration beaded his brow, and he was breathing very hard and fast.

"We saw him going around the corner and in the back way," I said. "There wasn't time to call the police. We'll call them now." I noticed Nancy had already gotten rid of her branch, so I leaned my pipe against a storefront.

"Not yet. We don't have any evidence," Nick objected.

"He pulled a gun on you! What do we need, a corpse?"

"I want to hang around and see who else shows up. Conan and Maria didn't know I knew I was Frageau. That really threw them. If they're in this with Boisvert and Lingini, why didn't they know? Boisvert knows I'm on to him. My phone call to Paris tipped him off if he didn't suspect already. He'd have been in touch with his wife."

"Yes, and his friend's attempt to kill you confirms it," I added. The speed walking was getting to me. I was gasping for breath. "Where are we going, to your car?"

"Too obvious," he muttered, and looked up and down the street for inspiration, but we kept walking back toward the car. Nick jiggled assorted car door handles as we went. He stopped at a black Fiat that the driver had left unlocked and opened the door.

"We can't do this!" I exclaimed, already doing it. "What on earth will we say if the owner comes out?"

"We tell him we made a mistake, thought it was our friend's car," Nick said, as though I were a lunatic for asking.

Nick was as nervous as a cat. He lit one of the awful Gauloises he'd been using to "age" the Frageau, and blew

the smoke out the window. We all sat staring at the mauve
door and the drawn blinds at the window. It took Boisvert
and his crooked-nosed henchman fifteen minutes to arrive.
It was the first time I had actually seen the elusive Boisvert.
He looked a little like de Gaulle, but shorter and altogether
less imposing, though he was half a foot taller than his
cooked-nosed friend.

"I thought Boisvert and Conan weren't working together," I reminded Nick.

"I only said Conan didn't know I knew I was Frageau.
They must be working together all right. Boisvert was just
holding out on them."

"You left the Frageau there, Nick!" Nancy exclaimed.

"That's the reason I went, to deliver the Frageau."

Boisvert knocked on the gallery door and Conan let him
and his friend in.

"The clan is gathering," Nick said, his eyes narrowed,
but I think it was the smoke from the Gauloise that caused
it.

"Too bad Interpol isn't gathering," I said. "Are we just
going to sit here and watch them all eventually disperse?"

Nick looked at me hopefully. "You wouldn't happen to
be an Interpol agent?"

"With these fingernails?"

Nancy came to attention. "I wonder if Bert is—Interpol,
I mean. Maybe that's why . . ."

A mangy black dog wandered by. "Or Fido might be an
agent," Nick said hopelessly.

I mentally finished Nancy's sentence. That's why Bert
wouldn't return to the States.

A short argument ensued, started by me. "I don't know
how you expected Interpol to come, Nick. The only person
you notified is Lingini."

"I don't know where Claude and Réné are staying."

"They're not Interpol."

"They didn't come with Boisvert," he pointed out
vaguely.

"Some catalyst. All that'll happen is that they'll take the

Frageau and run. Sell it for another fifty thousand and leave you in the lurch—till they find time to kill you."

"If they run, I'll follow."

"We have two guns," Nancy said. She took out Conan's with the silencer attached to the muzzle. I felt nervous, just being in the car with it, and told her to put it away. I was definitely not made for this adventurous life.

"We better go to your car, Nick, if you're planning to follow them," I said. Really the man was hopeless.

"There are keys in this Fiat," he replied.

Within thirty seconds, there was also an irate citizen with a briefcase at the door, demanding to know what we were doing in his car. Nick was the soul of charm. *"Scusi, signore."* He explained the "error." His friend had an identical car. We were to meet him, wait here. When we saw the keys in the ignition . . . The man *hmphed*, threw up his hands, used the words, *"polizia"* and *"ladro"* (thief) a couple of times, then melted into smiles when Nancy unfolded herself from the backseat. Eventually the man left in his Fiat.

"Still no Interpol," I worried. And still no commotion from behind the mauve door of the Minosi Gallery. The curtains remained closed.

As we all stood looking at the door, a motor scooter pulled up. The driver was not immediately recognizable, but beneath the black helmet there hung a black beard, and when Bert removed the helmet, we saw his moustache was in place as well.

For a wild instant I thought Bert *was* an Interpol agent. What did I really know about him? He'd left Troy eight years ago. He'd been all around the world since then. A tour guide would make a good cover for an international agent, and Bert had always had devious twists in him. It was no mistake he had fallen into the Tiber and been saved from drowning by Nick. He had arranged it, as he had arranged a job at the Risorgimento. Probably he had even arranged to meet Conan and Maria. And now he was here, to save our bacon.

He lifted the visor of his helmet and said, "So what's

going down here, folks? I decided to drop by on my way to the hotel."

My vision faded. Bert Garr an Interpol agent? Sure, and I was Mata Hari.

"All hell's breaking loose," Nick told him. "They're all in there. Conan pulled a gun and was going to kill me."

"Conan?" Bert looked like a frozen fish, eyes goggling.

"He was the first one to arrive."

"I'm gone. I'm history. You didn't see me."

"Bert, you chicken!" Nancy exclaimed. "Lana and I went in and rescued Nick. We're women! Are you going to run away from trouble all the rest of your life?"

"You got it." He pushed the helmet in place, stepped on the pedal and roared away. One corner of the beard had come loose and was flapping in the wind.

Nancy gave a disgruntled look and said, "My hero."

"We should have asked him to call the police," I said. "Nick, you'd better call them."

Bert's conscience, or maybe his wish to redeem himself in front of Nancy, got the better of him. He turned around and came rushing back. "Want I should send the cops?" he hollered.

I said, "Yes!"

"We wouldn't want you to put yourself in too much danger," Nancy snipped.

Bert looked like a dog that had been whipped. His face was red, but as he hadn't been lying, I assumed it was shame. He didn't answer her, but he didn't leave. While he sat there on the bike, trying to decide what to do, a big white Bentley pulled up in front of the Minosi and stopped, right in the middle of the road. A band of men with guns jumped out, and in the center of the small army strode Contessa Lingini, fashionable as ever in white linen slacks and a brothel red top, cut in a low *V* in the back. In her manicured fingers she carried a dainty little pistol. Another car, an ordinary red Fiat, roared up behind it and Claude and Réné got out.

Lingini tossed her head and one of the men tried the door knob. When it didn't open, he put his shoulder to it and broke it down, just like in the movies. Lingini strolled in as calmly as if she owned the place. We all looked at each other in confusion. "Maybe I should go and help her?" Nick asked doubtfully.

I held his arm. "Let's wait and see if there's shooting. We don't know why she's here."

There was no shooting. The first to emerge from the door, about five minutes later, was Conan, held down on either side by Lingini's armed men. His arms were pulled behind his back. Boisvert and his crooked-nosed friend were next, Claude was minding Boisvert, Réné in charge of the other. Last came Maria, with Lingini's long fingernails pinching into her upper arm in a way that would leave bruises. In her other hand, Lingini carried the Frageau. It was wrapped again in Nick's wrapping paper.

Lingini spoke to one of the men, who stayed behind at the shop with the broken lock. The rest of them piled into the two cars, and as quickly and quietly as they had arrived, the cars zoomed away. The people passing on the sidewalk hardly even glanced at the drama.

"Is this okay?" Bert asked in confusion.

Nick hunched his shoulders "Who knows? The Contessa could be Interpol, or she could be . . ."

"Holy Christ! You mean—the mob?"

Nick hunched his shoulders again. "She must be one or the other, don't you think?" he asked doubtfully. "Such a public display of force . . ."

Bert looked at Nancy. She looked a challenge at him. "Maybe we'd better follow that blonde," Bert decided, and revved up the motorcycle, but he kept several car lengths behind.

"Hop in," Nick invited, and we wedged into the Alfa-Romeo. He turned the key; the motor didn't make a sound. Dead as a doornail. Nick kept turning the key and pressing on the gas. In frustration he added the persuasion of a fist to the dashboard dials. Eventually he remembered. "It seems we're out of gas," he said sheepishly.

"And Bert's following them all alone!" Nancy wailed.

"He thinks we're following him. Oh Nick, you've got to *do* something. Steal a car. Do *something*."

He pulled out his gun and ran down the street, trying car door locks again. A driver pulled into the curb. "Police. I have to commandeer your car," Nick said, flashing his wallet. In the confusion he spoke English. I saw the edge of his American Express card, looking not at all like a badge, but the female driver was so excited she just stood aside and let him jump in. The car had no back door. I hopped in front, Nancy ended up sitting on my knee in the front seat. Nick already had the car moving, and we had to get in as best we could.

The road was thick with traffic. The only way we could keep an eye on our quarry was by Bert's motorcycle, which we spotted weaving in and out between cars. When we got into heavier traffic, Nick took to the sidewalk for a whole block. It is a very strange experience to drive fast in a car with a fully grown woman sitting on your lap so that you can't see anything, but can hear the horn blasting a long, continuous hoot. From the side window I saw bewildered people staring at us, giving a comprehensive Roman shrug that is a mixture of mild surprise and resignation.

"They're going to the Contessa's place," Nick announced.

"Is it safe to follow if they're the mob?" I asked. "I mean, what can we actually do?"

"Bert is still with them," Nancy said in a voice that overrode any further objection.

I understood from Nick and Nancy that the Contessa's Bentley and the red Fiat had roared into the Contessa's driveway. I wouldn't know. All I could see was trees. I was pretty busy trying to keep Nancy's hair out of my mouth, and my legs from falling asleep.

We jolted to a halt across the street half a block away. Nick and Nancy jumped out. "Where's Bert?" Nancy asked, and began looking all around. "He was ahead of us. Did you see where he went, Nick?"

"He must be around here somewhere."

We watched as people began to stream out of the cars. It

reminded me of the circus, where a whole army of clowns exit from a mini car built for one. It was during the confusion of the exit that Conan made his move. Two men, not small ones, were holding his arms. Conan shook them off as if they were mosquitoes. His big hands rose and he banged their heads together.

In a flash, he took to his heels, down the driveway. The Contessa raised her gun and shot, but well over his head. She either didn't want to kill him, or was a terrible shot. Neither did she order her men after him. The two of them that Conan had disabled were picking themselves up from the ground. The others were fully occupied with Boisvert and his friend. She scanned the street for helpers, spotted Nick across the road and shouted to him to stop Conan. Conan took off in the other direction.

Nick, to do him justice, ran after the raging bull, but there were several yards between them, and Conan was in better shape than Nick. We then learned where Bert was hiding. There was a roar of engine and his motorcycle shot out from the shrubbery a few yards beyond the Contessa's villa. He looked frightening in his Darth Vadar helmet and with that black beard. I don't think Conan recognized him. He just gave one look over his shoulder as he ran. Bert made right for him. Conan zigged and zagged, and ran into the grounds of the next villa. There was a fence with iron palings that would prevent the motorcycle from following him. Bert stopped the machine and leapt off. I wouldn't have thought he could move so fast. He caught Conan by the seat of the pants just as he was about to vault over the iron palings.

He caught Conan off balance and pulled him to the ground, arms flailing. Bert's I mean. It must have given him a great sense of satisfaction to hit Conan, though I don't think the blows did much damage. It was Nick and Nancy, rushing forward with guns drawn, who stopped Conan from retaliating. I was rushing, too, sans gun. I doubt if either of them would have shot except in case of dire necessity.

The Contessa came running down the street, led by her pack of pit bulls. She must have released them while we weren't looking. The air was rent with their yapping. They were well trained. At her command, they went for Conan. There was a confused mêlée of beige and gray and black squirming bodies leaping all over him. I counted six, although it was hard to do a good count—they were so active, darting here and there, trying to find a leg or arm to attach their teeth to. Bert got up and beat a hasty retreat to safety. When Conan was subdued, the Contessa whistled and the dogs released him. She had her gun trained on him.

She said a few words to Nick, then walked off, cool as a cucumber, with Conan in front of her, her muzzle in his back. We all stood around at the car Nick had comandeered.

"Oh Bert, you were so brave," Nancy said, and threw herself into his arms. She was crying from joy.

Bert gave a modest smile. "What goes around, comes around. Nick saved my life. Happy to be able to return the favor," he said.

"Thanks, buddy." Nick grinned. "I owe you one."

No one was so gauche as to intimate Bert hadn't exactly saved Nick's life. The important thing was that he had redeemed himself in his own and Nancy's eyes. It had taken real courage to tackle Conan, and in the pinch, he had done it. Already he looked better, more sure of himself, more mannish. I should have been feeling conscience qualms about doubting Bert, but I was so happy for him that all I felt was relief, and happiness.

"I wasn't going to miss the chance of having that guy locked up," Bert said. "I hope I blackened his eye. I sure as hell broke my knuckles." He examined his bruised fist, blowing air on it to cool it.

"Do we know for sure he *will* be locked up? I mean, there was some question whether the Contessa is Interpol or the mob," I mentioned.

"Interpol," Bert said. "I crouched behind the bushes for a few minutes. Heard the guys talking. One of them— Claude, it was—asked Lingini if she was sure she didn't want the prisoners taken to H.Q. She said no, her place was closer, and she wanted to question them before she turned them over."

"She showed me her identification," Nick corroborated. "She's going to call me later in the day, when she's taken care of Boisvert and the others. She's a little busy right now. Shall we go?"

Bert looked at his knockoff Gucci. "Holy cow! I'm late for work. I'll be in touch with you guys later. Hey, why don't you come down to the Risorgimento with me? We'll do lunch."

"First we have to return this stolen car," I reminded Nick.

"Where's the Alfa?" Bert asked.

"It's out of gas," Nick said with an annoyed *hmph*, as though it were the car's fault.

"So what else is new?" Bert laughed.

He put on his helmet and went to pick up the motorcycle. As he drove past, he shouted, "I'll call a garage."

He hadn't done a single bit of boasting about his heroism. That was unlike Bert. Rich men didn't have to dress up, he'd said. Maybe heroes didn't have to boast.

"That Bert, what a guy!" Nick said. "He actually went after Luigi."

"If the Contessa is an agent, how come she didn't have cuffs on Luigi?" Nancy asked.

"They didn't fit. His wrists were too big. Imagine." He looked wistfully at his own slender wrists and delicate hands.

"Never mind, Nick," I consoled. "They couldn't get them on Luigi, and they wouldn't be able to keep them on you. You could slip right out of them."

"Is that another put-down, Lana?"

"Put-down? *Moi?*"

CHAPTER 17

Our second visit to the Villa Lingini occurred at four o'clock on that same afternoon. In the interim we had returned the borrowed car, got Nick's car gassed up, and driven to the terrace of the Risorgimento to see Bert. He was there with his phony beard removed. "I got rid of the hair. Won't be needing it with Conan behind bars. The boss complimented me. You guys are late," he said. "Italian traffic—Dante's Inferno revisited. I was fifteen minutes late for work myself. Pietro didn't care for that." He wet the end of his pencil with his tongue, pulled out his order pad and said, "Campari and soda for starters, folks?"

"Perrier for me," I said. The others ordered the same.

Since the food at the Risorgimento was so awful and Bert was too busy to talk much, we decided to eat elsewhere. We went to Carlo's in the Piazza Mastai, for the hasty noon meal they call *pranzo*. As the sun rose high, the better to find us and blast us with heat, we went back to Nick's place. The Contessa called and invited him to the villa to explain the details.

I had to admit there was more to her than fingernails and designer gowns. Some corner of her psyche must have become bored with the mindless social whirl, and her aging conte. What an enviable life she led, surrounded by all that Italian grandeur, and topped off with a title. She was the sort of lady Nick would marry one day. I knew why she was inviting him to her villa. She probably already had his bride picked out for him, one of her gilded friends. Or maybe she meant to keep him as her own boyfriend on the side. That husband was no prize.

"What time do you think you'll be back?" I asked diffidently. Our adventure was really over now, and the sooner we rejoined our tour, the sooner I could begin to mend my cracked heart.

"It wasn't a dinner invitation. We'll probably only stay half an hour. You're both invited, of course," he said matter-of-factly.

He'd never know how my heart soared at the news, and how hard I had to work to answer with equal blandness, "Oh, really? I guess that'll be all right, huh, Nancy?" She nodded.

"Bert should be home soon. We'll wait for him," Nick said. "I told her an hour."

This gave Nancy and me time to refurbish our wilting appearance. Competing with a cosmopolitan contessa on her own grounds was futile. We opted for youthful American, Nancy in a pair of flowered jams and white shirt, I in a black and white flowered sundress. Of course I noticed immediately that Nick had shaved and put on a clean shirt and a light-weight suit.

"I didn't realize it was formal!" I said.

He looked self-conscious. "She's a contessa after all. But you look fine. She knows you're Americans," he added.

"We'll remember not to snap our bubblegum," I said, ostensibly to Nancy, but of course for Nick's benefit.

"Bert's washing up," he said. "He should be down any minute."

As soon as Bert came down, spiffy in a clean shirt and wearing a jacket, we left. On this visit, we got into the room with all the white and blue pottery. It held lots of other collectibles as well. Eighteenth-century chairs done in needlepoint, Persian rugs, Delft urns in faience, barrels of fresh flowers, Fabergé eggs. That kind of thing. The room was the size of a blowing alley. The Contessa hadn't bothered to change to entertain the riffraff. The pack of pit bull terriers patrolled outside the French doors, lending a homey touch.

She served thimbles of sweet, strong espresso from a toy silver pot, with no offer of cream. We all declined the gooey cake that accompanied the espresso.

"I thought you might be curious as to the finalizing of the case, Niccolò," she said. She had garnered Nick on the sofa beside her. "I'm afraid I'll be reneging on that offer to buy the Frageau. Charming as it is, it doesn't fit my collection. I collect late nineteenth-century works." She waved a hand vaguely at the Van Gogh. "And, of course, the Picasso in the front hall that Pablo gave me. Claiming to want a Frageau was merely my entrée to the syndicate."

Bert's eyes bulged and a strangled gasp escaped his lips. My own stomach began doing flip-flops at the sinister word.

"Not that syndicate," she assured us. "Luigi Mineo and Boisvert are rather small potatoes, really. French Interpol was investigating Boisvert vis-à-vis the Frageau scam."

"Edouard Fargé tipped them off, I suppose?" Nick asked.

A polite frown puckered the Contessa's brow. "Who is that? I don't recognize that name."

Nick launched into a long exposition of the story Claude and Réné had told him about the drowned body.

"Ah, Claude and Réné." She waved a dismissing hand. "How imaginative the French are. French Interpol sent them to assist me. I had no use for them. They were mucking about, muddying the waters. Is that what they told you?" She gave a disdainful shake of her head. "Pure fabrication, but they had to say something when you overtook them. They phoned me from the Risorgimento the other day, when they were following Boisvert. I told them to do nothing, say nothing. In fact I dashed down to the hotel immediately to make sure they left—and to see what *you* were up to," she added with a coquettish smile.

"About Fargé," Nick prodded.

"There was no Fargé in the case," she said. "That was pure fabrication, a clumsy effort to keep you from thinking you were under any cloud of suspicion."

Nick's Latin blood simmered. "Why should I be? I'm the victim!"

The Contessa took the global view. "The whole world of art is the victim in matters of this kind. Patrons become leary of buying for fear they're being cheated, and the dealers suffer in consequence. It was the purchase of a forged Corot by my husband that first got me involved with the Art and Fraud Squad. Poor Roberto, he knows so little of art. I could have told him it was a forgery if he had spoken to me before buying. Corot was prolific—three thousand paintings, more or less. But there are ten thousand 'Corots' in France alone.

"But you're not interested in my dull story," she said modestly. "It was the noted French collector, Pierre Duplessis, who first alerted us to trouble in the Frageau case. He bought a Frageau from Boisvert, and wanted more. He is very greedy, that Duplessis. He has eleven Renoirs, imagine! Boisvert hedged, and finally said the artist had moved to Italy. He had lost contact with him. Duplessis is like a bulldog. He said he would institute inquiries in Italy. Suddenly Boisvert remembered Frageau was dead. It was enough to rouse Duplessis's suspicions. He spoke to friends at *Art World* magazine. He had induced them to do a story on Frageau to increase the value of his paintings. They told him Conte Braccio had bought a Frageau from the Minosi Gallery in Rome recently, which suggested the artist was still alive."

"How did Luigi Mineo get hold of a Frageau?" Nick asked.

"He has long arms, reaching into many countries and many rackets. Mineo began investigating when he learned Braccio wanted a Frageau. He soon learned the Frageaus came from Paris—Boisvert, to be precise. So Mineo went to Paris and spoke to Boisvert. You may be sure he did his homework first. He would have known there was no one named Frageau painting in Italy, and suspected a racket. He asked around Paris and someone came up with your name, Niccolò, so he had that knowledge to hold over Boisvert's head. Of course, each recognized the other for a scoundrel.

The criminal element, like the international art crowd, is a close fraternity. Mineo threatened that if Boisvert didn't come up with a Frageau, he'd report the whole thing. Boisvert had held on to a couple, waiting for the price to soar. Per force, he had to sell Mineo one, which he sold to Conte Braccio.

"Meanwhile Duplessis had drawn Interpol into it. They contacted me, I went to the Minosi Gallery and began establishing contact. More coffee, anyone?" She looked around at four full cups and continued.

"I cultivated Mineo's girlfriend, Maria Bambolini. She has social ambitions. I told her I was eager to acquire a Frageau. My interest in Frageau led me to you, Niccolò, and, of course, your agent." She smiled at Bert, who preened. "I learned Maria had been seeing an American art dealer, whose sole artist had lately come from Paris. Mineo is heartless. He used that stupid cow, Bambolini, like a counter in his games. It was her role to entrap you, Mr. Garr, and get her greedy little hands on any stray Frageaus that were hanging about."

"She didn't mention Frageau to me," Bert said.

"She wouldn't. They're not amateurs! She hoped to find where the Frageaus were, and help herself to them."

"Why did Mineo keep beating up on me, if he set Maria on me in the first place? He seemed sore as a boil," Bert said, in forgivable confusion.

"He has his reputation to maintain. Maria is his woman. Naturally he had to make some show of protecting her honor. Also it made a good pretext to follow you about, in hopes that you'd lead him to the Frageaus."

Her attention soon returned to Nick. "At first," she confessed playfully, "I suspected you were in on the racket, Niccolò. Playing dead, and meanwhile painting the odd Frageau for your friends. There were rumors of two new Frageaus on the market."

"They're not new," Nick told her. "They're old. I brought them from Paris with me. They were stolen from my villa, by Boisvert's man."

"Ah yes, Boisvert brought an accomplice to Rome with

him. He was worried when the story broke in *Art World*, of course, and came looking for you. I shouldn't be at all surprised if he planned to harm you," she said nonchalantly.

"The gun shots in my car led me to the same suspicion. I would have appreciated it if you'd dropped me a hint, Rosa," Nick said politely.

A cool tinkle of laughter rippled from her lips and she wagged one of her long fingers with the bloodred tip at him. "But then I wasn't quite certain you were innocent, Niccolò. When I went to your exhibition and saw those lovely tempera paintings, I felt you were not the sort to connive with Mineo. Still, those two Frageaus surfaced. Mineo knew I was after one, and had Maria put out feelers to me. He and Boisvert must have come to some sort of terms, though Boisvert still planned to double cross him. Mineo never did produce the Frageau. He just told me he had a line on two. Boisvert kept them from him. We found the two in Boisvert's hotel room, by the by. You'll get them back eventually. They're being held as evidence."

"And the one I delivered to the Minosi Gallery today?" he asked. "The one you carried off."

"That, too. It's being fumigated. Really, those Gauloises! An amateur's way of aging, Niccolò. You painted that to stir up the hornet's nest. Rather dangerous. Boisvert went to the Minosi Gallery this morning with the intention of killing you."

"Why did Luigi notify him I was there?"

"He planned to attempt some blackmail. I expect he would have made Boisvert hand over the two Frageaus he had, or he'd threaten to call the police and reveal everything he knew—with you in person to substantiate it. He wouldn't have done it, of course, but it was a good threat. I imagine they would have killed you, if Boisvert had knuckled under to the threat. Boisvert would have made that his term of acceptance. While you were alive, he was in imminent danger of being exposed for the vile vermin he is. You shouldn't have gone barging in there alone. You might better have confided in me."

"I wasn't sure you were quite innocent either, Rosa."

"Touché. It was fortunate you called me, in any case. You didn't know my reputation, then? I was afraid, when you called, that my doing the odd job for Interpol had become public knowledge," she explained.

"I suspected you might be with Interpol," he said.

"I would appreciate it if you not bruit it about town. I'm presently involved in a rather important case—some ancient Egyptian artifacts that have been smuggled to Roma. You'll be required to give evidence in the Frageau case, but there's no reason *my* name must surface. I'll see that you recover all the money from Boisvert, if he hasn't spent it, or got it smuggled into a Swiss account. In any case, this sort of notoriety will do your reputation any amount of good."

"Notoriety!" Nick exclaimed in high dudgeon.

Her hand found its way to his arm and gave a reassuring squeeze. "Those of us who matter will know the truth, Niccolò. There is no denying the general public will misunderstand and believe you are a crook. They like that sort of thing in America. You'll find, I suspect, that your Frageaus are in higher demand than your real art."

Bert's eyes wore a conniving expression. I foresaw him urging Nick to paint more Frageaus. But when he spoke, it was about something else. "Who disabled Nick's car at the Forum last night, Contessa, and why?"

"That was Claude. Since he and Réné were in Rome, I used them to keep an eye on you and Boisvert, to give them something to fill their reports. It is all *tapisserie* in France, you know—red tape. Claude was watching your house, and followed you to the Forum. He phoned me to learn where Boisvert was. We had some little fear Boisvert might succeed in killing you, Niccolò. But I knew from Réné that Boisvert was with Luigi Mineo at the time. Claude wasn't supposed to let you know you were being followed. I told him to come here, planning to give him a good lecture. I also told him to fix your car so you couldn't follow him here. As Claude and Réné had revealed themselves to you, that would only alert you that I was Interpol. I wasn't sure I wanted you to know that."

We soon left, before she could foist any more espresso on

us, and went out to the Alfa-Romeo. It had a ticket stuck under the broken windshield wiper. Nick removed it and put it under the wiper of the car behind him.

Bert leaned over Nick's seat and said, "We're sitting on a gold mine here, my man. You did that Frageau in four hours. Four hours—and God only knows what price it'll fetch now that you're notorious."

"I am *not* notorious! I'm a respectable artist."

"Respectable artist—a contradiction in terms, Nick. Like a virgin whore. The worse your reputation is, the better they'll like you. Look at Van Gogh—slicing off his ear for some hooker."

"For Gauguin," Nick corrected.

"You're kidding! You mean he was a perv?"

"No, it wasn't like that."

"Wouldn't surprise me. Goya was a regular sleaze. And I'm pre-tty sure old Michelangelo liked the ladies—or maybe it was the men. They're all perverts. Man, you'll make the cover of *People* magazine."

"My father will kill me," Nick said weakly, and put his head on the wheel of the car. Then he lifted it and smiled. "But Mama will be happy. She likes scandal."

Rome was reawakening from its interminable coma, which they jokingly call the lunch hour, when we coasted down the hill, into the lethal traffic of the inner city.

"Tonight we celebrate!" Nick decided.

But "tonight" was a few hours away, and first we celebrated at an open café, drinking the Castelli white wine that rushed to the head, inducing a delightful giddiness.

Giddily, we discussed the past few days, and attempted to clarify any little confusion that lingered.

"She thought I was a crook," Nick kept saying, shaking his head sadly. "She," of course, was the Contessa.

"Nothing personal. Mistrusting people's her business," Bert explained. "She liked you. Better than Maria liked me. I'm the one that was used. I hope they lock Conan up tight for a couple of decades."

"And Boisvert," Nick added. "I trusted that man. He was

like a father to me. He called all his artists his sons, unless they're women, of course. Then he called them 'cherie.' "

The voices became whispers on the wind, breezing past my ears. Across the street, old and crumbling medieval buildings hunkered together, as if guarding some ancient secret. Disinterested pedestrians jostled along, ignoring the lost waif tourists. I felt the cooling benediction of the *ponentino* against my brow, the westerly wind from the distant sea that rescues you just when you think you can take no more heat. Traffic wheeled by. More pedestrians, obviously Romans, launched unconcernedly into its perilous flow. Horns blared. Fists rose and shook in mock anger. Rome was a mock city, half show, half museum. That was its secret. Its inhabitants were all actors, enjoying the role of Roman citizens. I smiled bemusedly at this insight.

When we left the café and Nick cut into a line of fast-moving traffic, my knuckles did not turn white. No knot hardened in my stomach. I had become acclimatized to Rome. I turned a dismissing, Roman blank-eyed look on the performing traffic policeman in his white helmet and gloves.

We took our siesta late, but we took it. Nancy and I went up to our room at the villa.

"Has Bert said anything about going back to the States?" I asked. She knew what I meant: Has he proposed?

"He said he often thinks about it." She was answering the question asked, not the one meant. "He'd like to go back, but he says he can't. He has his work here—Nick's beginning to make it big. Bert's approaching thirty. He thinks he'll be behind all the gang he went to school with if he goes home. You know, starting out somewhere like a kid fresh out of high school, probably working for someone younger than he is. He only has a high school education."

"He has a lot of foreign travel experience," I said. "He speaks some Italian and French."

She just looked. We both knew how limited the demand was for foreign tongues in Troy. "He'd never get a decent job at home. And what could I do in Rome?" she asked in a perfectly rhetorical manner.

"I love Rome. I wish I could stay."

"Did Nick say anything?"

"He said he couldn't stand our winters."

"Hmph. Maybe if you changed your hair . . ."

As this conversation was only depressing the hell out of us, we lay down and closed our eyes and pretended we were resting. At seven-thirty we got up and dressed for the celebration dinner. I didn't feel a single wince when we left the room in an utter shambles. What had happened to me?

Dinner wasn't till nine, and probably wouldn't end till midnight. In an effort to make the evening enjoyable for us, Nick and Bert chose a restaurant designed for tourists. It was neither theater nor museum, but an international, high-priced place in the Trastevere, where the waiters spoke English. Oh, they acted Italian for the customers, with their beaming smiles and balletic hands and pirouetting feet, but they didn't fool me. This wasn't the real Rome. The service was too good. The waiters were too polite. I felt gypped.

The fettucini was fresh, the clam sauce was fine, and the wine was better than average, served in earthenware amphorae. Other pseudo Italian touches abounded—plaster busts of emperors on plaster columns, imitation fresco murals in the style of Raphael, and lots of antipasti. We all tried very hard to be high-spirited, but it was about as enjoyable as a baby's funeral. A pall hung over our table, punctuated by occasional efforts at gaiety on the part of whoever had the ambition to tell a joke, mostly Bert.

I looked at the other customers, tourists like me and Nancy, except that they thought this was the real Rome. Even the music was tourist style. They played "Isle of Capri" and "That's Amore," and a black-haired young man sang one verse in Italian to lend a foreign air to it. When they struck up "Arrivederci, Roma," I couldn't stand it any longer. Unshed tears burned the back of my dry eyes. Nick hadn't said a word about the future.

We left before eleven. "We'll catch that eleven-fifteen bus to Salerno tomorrow morning," I said to Nancy, loud enough for everyone to hear. Nancy didn't answer.

Silence reigned in the backseat, except for a few soft

murmurings and the rustle of Bert's jacket as he got his arms around Nancy. My heart felt like a boulder, weighing me down. I refused to look out the windows at the lights of Rome. I just looked straight ahead through the windshield, watching the red lights of the car ahead of us, while the wind whistled through the bullet holes. I had no idea where we were going, but when Nick turned into a parking area beside the Tiber, I knew this wasn't the route to his house.

Bert came to life in the backseat. "A sentimental journey, you old sentimental son of a gun," he laughed. "This is where Nick hauled me out of the river—right at this piling, wasn't it, Nick?"

"This, or one like it," Nick said.

"I've got to see this!" Nancy said, and we all got out.

Below, the writhing bodies of an amorous twosome were sprawled over the bridge pier, ignoring the Tiber's roar a few feet away. The place was a lovers' lane, which made me wonder whether Bert had fallen out of a boat or been pushed in the drink by his girlfriend. I also wondered what Nick had been doing there. Bert took Nancy below to show her where Nick fished him out of the drink.

"You'd have to be Tarzan to get down there!" Nancy objected. She was wearing high heels.

"No Tarzan. Me Dante, you Beatrice," I heard Bert croon.

If she married him after that, she deserved him.

"Shall we walk along the river bank?" Nick suggested.

We walked, hand in hand, looking at the dark roll of water. "Father Tiber, to whom the Romans pray," Nick quoted.

"Is that Shakespeare?"

"No, Macaulay, from the *Lays of Ancient Rome*."

I suppressed the bad pun that immediately came to mind. "Pagans, praying to a river."

"Shall we say a prayer? Make our petition to Father Tiber?"

"I've already wasted my change in the Fountain of Trevi."

"Did you make a wish to come back to Rome one day?"

"I think that one's free. I wished for—" I had wished for an exciting, romantic holiday. They say you should be careful what you pray for. Your prayer might be granted. I should have included a note that I wanted the romance to outlive the holiday. I didn't know the Gods of the Fountains were so literal-minded.

His hand slid up my arm, and thence around my waist. Our hips jostled companionably as we strolled along in the moonlight. At least, I think there was moonlight, up above the lights of the city. "What did you wish for?" We stopped walking, and he gazed pensively at me, waiting for my answer.

"Money."

"A thoroughly modern, American wish. I wished for success."

"A thoroughly modern, universal wish."

"And love," he smiled softly.

"One out of two ain't bad."

"Oh, I plan to be successful yet." His dazzling smile hovered above me, insinuating, possessive, wary.

"You *are* successful!"

"Then I'm twice blessed. In love, *and* successful." A wary gleam shot from his eyes as he risked lowering his head for a kiss that let off fireworks inside me. But love is a weasel word. What it meant to him might be different from what it meant to me.

"That wasn't so bad, was it?" he asked gently, and laughed.

I laughed, too, nervously, and pulled away to continue our stroll. "You're like a porcupine!" he complained. "I'm trying to ask you to marry me, Lana."

To my infinite relief, I did not exclaim "Marry!" aloud, though the word reverberated like thunder in my head. I said, "Oh," rather vaguely. "And what about the winters?"

"They're much warmer here."

"I teach during the winter."

"It seems redundant, teaching English to people who speak English. In Italy, you could teach English to Italians. Much more sensible. We could live in America for three-quarters of the year. The way you like, in an old brick house. With two children, and a dog. I'd like that. A man needs roots. I shouldn't be pointing out the advantages to *myself*!" he exclaimed guiltily. "Bert said you're old-fashioned. You'd never marry a foreigner. But I'm only partly Roman."

I felt I was partly Roman, too. "Maybe half the year in the States," I said. "But could you paint there?"

"I can paint anywhere. America's beautiful. But I'd like to paint people now. I'd like to paint *you*, with your fierce school teacher's scowl, and your lovely Renaissance eyes. I've noticed short-sighted women have those sort of eyes."

I slid off my glasses, the better to reveal my lovely eyes.

"And I want to be near Bert at first, to see he doesn't display me in McDonald's," Nick continued. "He mentioned it last night. If Nancy marries him, she'll tone him down," he added. "He's my friend. I can't drop him now that my career is becoming worth his while. Has she said anything?"

"She'll say yes," I said.

"Eccellente." His words were a sibilant seduction in my ear. "I'll give them the new Frageau for a wedding gift. And you? Do you say yes, Lana?"

"What was the question again?"

He replied in Italian, with both hands, both lips—in fact the whole body, the way Italians speak. Being half Roman myself, I replied in the same vein. The Gods of the Fountains had understood after all. Rome had claimed a part of me for her own, and I had won the noblest Roman of them all, or at least the one I wanted.

LAWRENCE SANDERS